CROSSHAIRS
Rogue Drones

Pferron Doss

BookLocker

ACKNOWLEGEMENTS

To Wendy Doss, the pillar of my life, whom I've been married over forty years, for her endless encouragement. To my kids, that I have bounced ideas off at nauseum. To Jeanne Porter, "Moms," that I am so blessed to have in my life, for her ongoing support. To Garrett Romaine, my generous guide and friend who kept my story telling voice, giving the manuscript the life it deserves. To Andrew Gragg, who never fails to awe me with his immense artistic talent, and who designed my book cover

AUTHOR'S NOTE

Pferron Doss was one of those raring-to-go- drone enthusiast "wanna-be" pilots, only to open its box contents, charge the battery and watch it fly down the street, crashing some fifty feet atop a clump of pine trees. There it stayed some thirteen months until mother nature finally shook it from its grip. Watching his Saturday morning Westerns, he had a thought. It dawned on him that "there used to be a time when men stood back to back, took ten paces, turned and fired… now what if they sat on the comfort of their front porch and sent out a drone to do their shooting?"

Table of Contents

CHAPTER 1: A Familiar Sound

As the mid-afternoon sun rose high in the sky, dozens of various urbanites relaxed in Vilas Park. Dogs ran recklessly across the green grass, chasing Frisbees while barking excitedly. Kids played on structures, continually shedding clothes, shouting and laughing in the hot summer sun while their parents watched over them. The soccer fields hosted made-up games involving assorted balls and rules, with fist-sized rocks lined up to denote official lines. Honored citizens played chess at their usual tables, half-heartedly arguing politics and lamenting the shortcomings of the younger generation. Across a small ravine, at two dilapidated tables underneath the shadows of the trees, a small group of young men lounged insolently, surveying their self-appointed turf. A smaller group of teenaged girls stood off to the side, talking quietly among themselves.

Out in the sunlight, a teenaged African-American male assembled a remote-controlled helicopter, checked his controller, and looked around. Miles Watson was seventeen years old, a senior at the local high school, and one of those kids who never fit neatly into the usual cliques at school. He was athletic, but not really interested in sports, and he was smart enough to do well at his studies if he chose to try, which he sometimes did not. He was good-looking, with short black hair, clear skin, easy smile, and clever eyes. Even dressed in faded jeans and a plain blue tee-shirt, he appeared to come from a good family. Assured that he had space to fly his 'copter, he started it up and launched it skyward.

Several onlookers turned simultaneously to the new sound. The small engine wasn't quiet, but it didn't shriek or pierce the air; it had a pleasing hum. As he performed cutting-edge aerobatics that only the very experienced could do, he soon was lost in an aerial trance. His face grew expressionless as he put the tiny craft through a series of moves, arcing and zooming through the summer sky. He was oblivious to the world around him; his focus went completely to his controller. When a swarm of gnats discovered his slightly sweaty face, he was brought back to reality, and he set the 'copter to hover while he brushed the bothersome bugs away.

His gaze followed the path of his helicopter as he banked in a wide loop, and out of the corner of his eyes, he saw the teens at the table in the shade. His body tightened, and his facial expression turned from clear joy to disdain. They seemed to be mocking him, making exaggerated robot motions with their hands on invisible controllers much like his. He glared back at the group, especially the one individual with daring baggy pants in great danger of falling off. A husky, muscled twenty-three-year-old African-American male was wearing dark shades, sported gaudy jewelry hanging off his neck over a bright white party shirt, and he was intricately tattooed on his neck and arms.

"Crap, it's Adam Jacobs," Miles said under his breath. He never called the young tough "AJ" because he knew it bothered him. Miles tried to return to his flight practice, but he was losing his concentration. The girls behind Adam were quite cute, he decided, variously sporting hair in cornrows or tight bobs, and all three wearing their blouses half-buttoned, with plenty to look at. They wore cutoff shorts, and their long legs were strong and athletic. He frowned, wondering how someone like Adam always managed to surround himself with the pretty ones. He shrugged, reminding himself that these were the same girls that always laughed and teased him as he rode his bicycle. Now, his only recourse was to put on a flying exhibition that would leave everyone speechless.

"Hey, AJ look at that! He's hell o good," one of the young males in the crew insisted. They all looked up, including AJ, who was attempting to talk business with his homies. AJ quickly became perturbed.

"Nah, anyone can fly them helicopters. His moves are pretty weak," AJ insisted with authority.

"I dun-no AJ, looks pretty hard to me," the teenager said slowly, staring as the helicopter continued to do aerials.

With that, AJ got up. "Shut the hell up! You don't know what you're talking about," he snapped with a loud voice while rising up to his full height. As he glared at each and every one around him, he saw that he regained their entire attention.

"So, what are those moves that dude is doing now? Looks pretty impressive to me," another broke in weakly, while taking a quick look over his shoulder.

Looking skyward and just shaking his head, AJ paused. "It's called a funnel, and I bet he'll attempt to roll out of it and fly into a pie dish."

A chuckle rang out from the group. "Pie dish? I'm hungry. Pass me some chips over here." This brought a deep scowl from AJ, who continued to glance up at the flying exhibition.

"Like I was saying. Watch this. He's flying his helicopter sideways in a circle nose, pointing it straight to the ground in a big olé' loop," he continued, while impressing his boys.

"I didn't know you could fly AJ," a follower shouted out with half-eaten chips hanging on his lips.

Motioning for one of the females to get him a beer, AJ waited until it was opened and handed to him. Alcohol was banned from the park, but AJ was never one to let rules interfere with his plans. "There's a lot you don't know about me," he grunted, licking his lips after a huge gulp.

"So, what's he doing now?" asked the tallest girl.

"He's setting up to go vertical for a tail spin," AJ said. "I bet he'll take it as high as he can, with the nose still pointing up and the fuselage almost parallel to the ground." He tried to sound bored. "Then..."

"Whoa, break it down, big guy," said one of the boys. "Us homies don't know the lingo."

AJ pounded his fist on the rickety picnic table and made it shudder. "Shut up and watch! It's falling out of the sky tail first. If he's half the pilot he thinks he is, he'll let it fall and not pull it out until it almost slams into the ground." A few seconds later the helicopter did exactly as he predicted.

Now the team was more impressed with AJ than with Miles. "You nailed it for sure," the tall girl said with astonishment. "Not bad, not bad."

Miles brought the helicopter back to his feet and cut the power; the blades whirred slowly to stop. Without fanfare, he next launched his airplane, a tiny blue fixed-wing model that resembled a common Cessna. It roared to life with a louder, more powerful whine, and immediately gained altitude and speed. Miles let it circle above him to ensure it was running properly without needing adjustments.

"AJ, AJ, there he goes again. Looks like a plane," the tall girl said. She pointed to the sky while pulling her braids out of the way.

"I can see and hear it. He's only doing basic rolls close to the ground," AJ said, taking another long swig from his beer and tossing aside the can. "Hope he crashes it. Someone hand me another beer!" he commanded.

By this time the plane was high in the sky and climbing to the point of stalling, then smoothly leveled out. Miles again glanced back over to the group and took both hands off the transmitter. The plane continued to fly away, with the noise noticeably fainter. When the sound was barely audible, he placed both hands back on the transmitter pushed a couple buttons. The plane adjusted course instantly and soon reappeared, to the amazement of the group.

"Wow, that's pretty cool. No hands driving, I meant flying," the jokester in AJ's posse marveled.

"That's nothing," AJ said, waving his hand. "All he did was push a button on the transmitter called a 'return to home' function. Hell, anyone can do that, even you, stupid!" he said, punching the jokester on the shoulder to add emphasis. The disciple rubbed his shoulder thoughtfully and moved a few steps away.

CHAPTER 2: A Confrontation

The modest two-floor family home where Miles lived was close to the park. It was recently painted a pleasant light blue, and the bushes were trimmed with care. There were cracks in the sidewalk, and the summer heat had turned the lawn brown, but the house still looked comfortable. Three middle school boys were riding their BMX bikes in the street in front of the house when one pulled up and cocked his ear to the sky.

The noise from Miles' aircraft props caught the ears of Kenny, his younger brother. Kenny smiled broadly. A full head shorter than Miles, wearing a collection of summer-wear that was partially handed down, Kenny was dressed in short pants, a ragged Nike t-shirt, and Converse high-tops that had seen better days. His hair was also trimmed close like his older brother, and he also had the same handsome smile. Kenny had just begun to fill out, with muscle mass beginning show on his stocky frame. Over the summer he had grown three inches, complaining of late night cramps in his legs and a changing voice that sometimes cracked when he least expected it.

"Hey, Kenny, you hear that? Someone's flying across the park," said his friend Dontrelle, a small boy straddling a nice, chromed five-speed that perfectly fit him. The third boy, named Bo, pulled up on a much older bike that seemed to be held together with black and silver tape. Bo was even smaller, and followed Kenny's every move. He remained quiet, awaiting instructions.

"Yeah, I've been listening and I bet it's my bro," Kenny said proudly. He looked back over his shoulder and spotted the plane doing a roll. "Yep, that's my bro's RC!" he said, pointing, as it disappeared behind some trees.

Dontrelle nodded and then looked around. "Let's head over to the bike park and do some flying of our own, BMX-style," he said excitedly. "I got some moves to practice." He made his bike seem like a snorting horse, raring to head out, rocking back and forth expectantly.

Kenny had a far-away look in his eyes. He wanted to keep riding, but he was always interested in what his brother was doing. He looked in the direction the plane was following and saw it disappear into the sun's rays, then quickly fly back into focus. "Naw you guys go ahead, I'll catch ya later. I'm gonna go see what Miles is up to." He turned his bike around and pedaled furiously toward the far end of the park, while the other two boys rolled smoothly to the concrete ramps of the bike park.

Kenny put his head down and pumped hard, paying little attention to his path. When he looked up he saw he had interrupted a soccer game, and the boys immediately yelled at him to get off the field. This only ensured his increased speed, and as he darted around some hedges he could recognize the familiar silhouette of his brother.

"Miles!" he yelled, while looking up at the descending plane. Kenny made a bee-line for his older brother, taking a direct line that brought him straight through AJ and his homies. Yelling, they parted hurriedly, and one of them threw a beer can at him, which fell short. Coming to a sliding, grinning halt, Kenny sent a shower of dirt and rocks flying, drawing a scowl from his brother.

"What the hey!" Miles growled. "You trying to start something? Them aren't the dudes to mess around with, and you know that," Miles reminded him. Avoiding eye contact with the aggrieved party, Kenny and Miles stood in silence, looking up at the flying exhibition as the aerobatics continued.

Disregarding the admonishment, Kenny smiled. "Hey bro, you said the next time I saw you flying you'd let me fly, so here I am," he boldly stated.

Trying to ignore his little brother, Miles pumped more power to the plane, and it revved harder. As it abruptly turned around toward them, he inverted the wings, doing multiple rolls. He knew he wasn't going to be left alone until he let Kenny fly, so he shrugged his shoulders. "Look, if I let you fly, you promise to pay attention to what you're doing? This is my favorite plane and I don't want it smashed because you weren't paying attention. You understand?"

Unfazed, Kenny nodded and muttered "Yeah, yeah, I know," as he impatiently moved closer, while reaching out for the transmitter. They exchanged the controller, and soon both sets of eyes were critically following the plane as Kenny took it through some basic turns and a couple shaky rolls.

Miles was not happy. "Steady now, give it more power," he cautioned. "Ok, turn it around, it's getting away from you," he commanded sharply. The plane's hum was getting less distinct.

"I got it, let me alone. I got it," Kenny assured him confidently. The plane reappeared from the sun's glare.

For the next few moments the buzzing of the prop swelled in the summer sky. The two brothers elbowed each other and laughed easily, sharing their bond. Soon, Dontrelle and Bo appeared, stopping close by and straddling their bikes.

"Hey Kenny, good flying dude," Dontrelle called out. This caused a quick look around from Kenny, just long enough for him to lose contact with the plane. It was obvious he had become cocky and Miles sensed it as well.

The plane began to lose altitude and Miles attempted to grab the transmitter but missed. Kenny pulled away and regained control to avert a crash. The plane was too low to effectively turn around, but inexperienced as he was, Kenny attempted it anyway. Barely missing some trees, he made the turn, but as it was coming back it buzzed AJ and his onlookers, causing them to duck. This scared Kenny. He panicked and flew it into the ground between AJ and himself. Dust rose from the crash site and the air grew quiet and tense.

Flustered, Miles snatched the transmitter from Kenny and pointed to the plane. "Get over there quick and pick it up before they get it. I'll gather up the other stuff, now hurry."

But it was too late. The plane had already been picked up by the thug with the large bleach spot in his hair. He held the plane high in the air like a trophy, far above Kenny's reach. Everyone in AJ's crew was laughing at the scene. "Now don't let your little ass get whooped today, back off" he taunted, while looking around and laughing at the despair in Kenny's face.

Kenny attempted to jump but was knocked to the ground in defeat. "Best you crawl on away from here before I have to show you what we do with little assholes like you," the young tough mocked.

Kenny looked back at Miles then jumped again but was intercepted in midair and forced back to the ground with the wind almost knocked out of him. Feeling embarrassed, hurt and alone out of the corner of his eye he saw a fist-sized jagged rock right under his forearm. With contempt he reached for it, jumped up and with a mighty, well-aimed throw that brought back all of his years as a Little League pitcher, he let fly. The rock smacked his tormenter square across the side of the face, almost knocking him to the ground. Staggering, he immediately dropped the plane and reached for his bloody face.

When the boy saw blood on his fingers, he was enraged. "You little..." he blurted, but before he could attack Kenny, he was restrained by two of his cohorts. Some of his attempt to wrestle away was for show, but he really did seem to want a piece of Kenny. The two held him firm, and he settled down.

Miles reached the rowdy group and saw the bloody and swollen cheekbone of the attended target. He felt despair; this was not good. His brother was standing near him, chest heaving as he gulped air. His small fists were clenched, and he seethed with rage.

"Come on Kenny, let's get on home," Miles said gently, touching his brother's arm.

But this time someone else stood in the way impeding any effort to pick up the plane. "Boy, do you know who we are?" one of the agitators hollered.

"Yeah, I know who you are. You're the BBB's" Miles announced as he placed Kenny behind him. The group had started to encircle them. Staring directly at AJ and without pause, Miles continued. "You're Adam Jacobs, and you're the so-called leader. Please tell your homie to give me my plane back."

In unison, everyone gasped at this boldness. AJ was offended, and his eyes narrowed. "His name is Kondray. I'm AJ, and nobody calls me Adam unless they want to get jacked up by my boys and me."

Not to be deterred, Miles looked at the group in disdain. "Yeah, yeah, whatever. Just get out of the way so I can get my plane and leave you alone," he insisted.

"You don't understand. You hurt my boy, rather that little ass did. There's a price you have to pay. Because no one messes with one of my boys without repercussions."

"Pay for what? He shouldn't have snatched the plane in the first place. It didn't hit any of your so-called boys," seethed Miles. He turned and pushed the bleeding agitator backwards, which caused him to step on the plane. Immediately everyone laughed aloud. "Oops," Kondray said insolently, as he shrugged his shoulders.

"Looks like the fuselage is broke," AJ said in mock sorrow.

Miles made a fist, then relaxed slightly. "Come on Kenny, let's get home. We don't need that plane anyway."

AJ didn't like that move at all. "Hold it! What good is that plane to me? It's busted. So, what's that thing in your hands?" he asked with sarcasm.

"You know what it is. It's a transmitter," Miles spit out. "I've seen you flying before, and you aren't gonna get it either. I heard you used to be a good pilot and used to teach kids to fly until..." he trailed off, while putting his arm around Kenny and squinting against the sun's setting rays.

"Until what?" AJ demanded. Getting no response, his eyes glared as he motioned to his boys. "Get it," he commanded.

With silent menace, the group tightened its circle. Kondray reached into his back pocket, pulled out a knife and with eyes full of rage, he thrust it towards Miles but he missed his attended target.

Kenny cried out, as did Miles. Kenny staggered and his body went limp. His eyes stared out at his brother, begging for help as he fell backwards striking his head on a partially buried boulder. Moaning softly, Kenny lay motionless on the grown as blood seeped from his shirt.

"Damn, AJ, I didn't mean to stick the boy," Kondray stammered while staring at the blood-stained switchblade "I was only doing what you told us to do. That little shit stepped in front of me," he uttered defensively.

AJ composed himself while shaking his head. "I told you. I told you you'd have to pay. I told you to come work for me a million times. Now look what you made me do," he said mockingly, shaking his head. Looking first at his boys, then scanning his immediate surroundings, he turned his gaze back at Miles. The two boys glared at each other. AJ broke the spell and shrugged, looking over at Kondray and smiling.

"Come on boys, let's scoot," AJ said. "I'll deal with you later, dawg," he said with authority. They all scattered, leaving beer cans, food wrappers, and other litter behind. Kondray staggered away, holding his face, pleading with AJ for medical attention.

Miles held his brother's head in his lap as his eyes began to close then up at the fleeing gang. With contempt, he struggled to holler out an oath, but only a whisper came out of his mouth. "I'll get you for this AJ, if it takes the rest of my life," he vowed.

Hearing the commotion, a young mother came running with child in tow. She looked down, quickly gave her child to her husband, and immediately knelt down beside Kenny. She reached into her purse, pulling out a diaper. "My name is Mandy and I'm a nurse," she told Miles, as he gave way to her authority. "Here, move away and keep the boy's head off the ground," she told Miles.

"Hurry up. He's not going to bite you," she commanded. She pulled Kenny's shirt up and placed the diaper over the oozing wound. "Someone call 911 and tell them we need an ambulance here in the park," she commanded, but another onlooker was already pecking at his phone. He turned away and started blurting out their situation.

Looking into Kenny's half-opened eyes, she smiled. "It's ok boy, you're gonna be ok, now you keep your eyes on me," she continued. "Lucky it wasn't a gunshot," she assured him.

The distant sounds of sirens pierced the air and approached the park. They soon arrived on the scene, driving right up across the hard earth of the field to where everyone had gathered. Mandy informed the ambulance drivers what she had done and who she was. Soon the police arrived, their lights punctuating the darkening skies.

"Make way, make way," an officer ordered as the ambulance drivers rolled a gurney closer to Kenny, who was sprawled and motionless on the ground. The EMTs smoothly swooped in like angels of mercy, bracing and locking the gurney expertly.

"Lots of blood, Officer Stew," one of them said to the policeman.

Placing her hand on Miles' shoulder, Mandy softly assured him. "It's ok boy, move out of the way and let them do their work. Move now, so they can load him up and get him to Valley Central Hospital." Miles didn't say a word as he did what he was told.

The police officer opened up his notepad and clicked a pen. Known as "Officer Stew," his nameplate said "Stewart" on his uniform. He was an older white cop, a little too heavy around the middle, with a sad, seasoned look in his eyes. He looked around. asking if anyone had seen what happened.

An old man leaning against his cane motioned a spectator to get out of his way as he pushed and limped his way forward. It was the old man known simply as "Pops," and he had an authority to him. He was dressed neatly, sporting a bow tie, and his white hair set off a dark, wrinkled face. "I saw what happened, officer. Sure enough, damn hoodlums are always in this park making trouble. Used to be a nice place for families and kids but not anymore, with this stuff happening all the time."

Glancing down at the boy as they placed him on a stretcher, Pops frowned and continued. "Somebody yelled 'AJ' is what I heard, but I don't know who stabbed the boy. Somebody in that damned gang sure enough did it. Call themselves the Bunker Buster Boys, BBB. Yep, that's who done it. Always driving them jacked up cars, playing music you can hear a mile away," he snorted.

The officer looked up from what he was writing and looked at the ambulance, which was now slowly leaving the park, siren blasting the night. "Anybody see which way they went?" the cop asked.

The old man tamped his cane on the ground, then lifted it and attempted to point in the correct direction, but almost stumbled. Regaining his balance, he pointed the way. "It's not right," he complained loudly. "You all need to patrol this park more and keep them good for nothing gangs away from here," he bellowed. "They scurried off like slinking dogs, he said, continuing to point in the direction of flight. "Yeah, everyone knows this here park belongs to AJ and triple BBB's, that's for sure. Ain't nothing bad happens here without them being in the middle of it."

The cop shrugged and turned to Miles. "Where do you live, boy? Gather up your stuff and I'll take you home. There's nothing else you can do here. He'll be in good hands, so come on now let's get you and all your things together." Reluctantly, Miles slowly carried the bike over to the police car, and pushed it into the trunk. He returned to the broken plane and picked it up, noting the damage and wondered which would be easier to repair – the plane or his brother.

CHAPTER 3: A Long Way Home

It was both the longest and shortest car ride Miles had ever taken. As he prepared himself for how he was going to tell his parents what had happened, he went over the situation over and over in his mind. He saw every detail in slow-motion, and it was agonizing to realize he couldn't stop the memories flooding over. That part seemed to take forever. At the same time, it was a very short drive, and took no time to get home. Pulling up in front of the house, the officer told Miles to slow down as he'd walked him up to the house. "Take a breath, son," he said calmly.

But Miles was practically running. Once at the door, Miles burst in, yelling. "Mama, Mama! Come quick, Mama!" he blurted out.

Bernestine Watson turned the corner and saw the officer standing in the doorway. He noted her professional clothes, expensive haircut, and intelligent eyes, guessing she was an office worker about forty years old. She paused, scanned the room, then grew agitated. "Where's Kenny? Where's Kenny?" she called out sharply. "Oh God, my boy! What's happened to Kenny?" she blurted out, as tears swelled up in her eyes.

"Mrs. Watson, I'm Officer Stewart. There's been an accident in the park. Your son has been taken to Valley Central Hospital. I can take you and your son to the hospital if you like," he gestured with concern on his face.

"Does my husband Omar know what happened?" she asked, while grabbing her purse and sweater.

"Yes, he's already being dispatched to the hospital, so we had better go now" officer Stewart said as he backed out of the house while holding the door open for Bernestine and her son. They jumped in the car and quickly sped away, lights flashing but siren muted.

Arriving at Valley Central, Officer Stewart ushered them through the hallways and shook hands with Omar, who thanked him for bringing his wife and son to the hospital. About six feet tall, with freshly cut hair slightly tinged with gray, Omar was a commanding figure. He was older than his wife by several years, and his face showed more age and tension than it probably should. After a deep embrace of his wife, Omar stared at Miles, leaving many things for later.

"They just took Kenny into surgery a few minutes ago, and I haven't heard anything," Omar said. Shifting his attention now to Miles he immediately started to frown. "What the hell happened?" he asked. "Why didn't you watch after your little brother?" But before Miles could say one word, his father continued with his rant. "I told you not to go down to that park anymore. That damn park hasn't been safe since them gangs done started taking over that place. It isn't safe for anyone to be there and we just don't have enough officers to patrol that park every minute of the damn day," he added, feeling somewhat guilty himself. "That's it! From here on out that park is off limits! You and your brother are no longer allowed to go to that park, you understand? Unless me or your mother are with you, I don't want you there!" said angrily.

Miles attempted to tell his dad what happened, but the emergency room door opened and in walked two, male doctors in their clean white lab coats. "My name is Dr. Jackson," said the older man, probably in his late forties, rubbing his chiseled face then his well-manicured beard while looking down at his clip board. "And this is Dr. Pope," he said politely, pointing to a wide eyed attentive intern with tightly braided cornrows and stylish glasses. They exchanged handshakes and pleasantries, and he grew serious. "Your son was brought in unconscious and we performed emergency surgery. Apparently, he was stabbed in the abdomen lacerating the liver and the trajectory was such it nicked the spleen" he said pointing to his side in an illustration. In addition, his head struck a rock and caused additional bleeding. We gave him a transfusion and got him stapled up. He was naturally in a lot of pain when he was brought in, so we gave him something for that. We performed a scan to ensure we didn't miss anything, and that was negative. I believe he will be ok after a few days. He's being taken up to recovery, and then to a room. You'll be notified what room he will be in at that time. Do you have any questions of me?" the doctor inquired.

"He'll be ok?" Omar said doubtfully.

Dr. Jackson nodded. "He's young and strong. It was a jagged wound, and there are no complications other than that spleen. We got that mended easily."

Miles hugged his Mom and she kissed him tenderly on the cheek, but said nothing.

"Ok then, why don't you all just have a seat in the waiting area? It'll be an hour or so before you can see your son." With that, both doctors went back into the emergency room, leaving the Watsons to talk.

Omar chose seats across the room from where everyone else had been sitting, as he didn't want their conversation to be interrupted by others seeking solace. With an unconcerned feeling towards Miles, he dug right in. "How many times have I told you to stop wearing that hoody? Pull up your pants and act like a decent kid! You can't even walk, your pants are so low, and you're gonna trip because you don't tie up those laces," he barked, baiting Miles for what was coming next. "Now tell me what happened and don't leave anything out," he demanded.

For the next thirty minutes Miles retold the story and started to cry when he informed his dad that Kenny wasn't the intended target. "He had stepped in between me and them guys. That knife was meant for me. I should have been the one stabbed, not him," he said with a heavy heart, while tears rolled down his face.

As Bernestine moved closer to Miles to comfort him, Omar became even more outspoken. "Don't you dare baby him! Had he

24

listened to me in the first place, this would have never happened! I told him to stay away from that park and to stop flying those airplanes and helicopters. So that's it! No more, and that's it!" Omar yelled, which turned everyone's attention toward him. At that point, Bernestine just shook her head at her husband.

Miles didn't want to hear that prohibition, as flying was his favorite escape from the living conditions in the crowded city and all the other teenaged angst in his life. Not having any place to go or hang out was bad enough. Flying was his only antidote from his loneliness. He had few friends, as many of the kids he grew up with had moved away when their parents relocated deeper into the suburbs after getting better jobs. Now everything was ruined. Nothing to do, and nowhere to go. He felt trapped.

Miles stood up and yelled back, "You want to change the neighborhood? Then you work in the park! That's where the gangs hang out. We have no place to go. You're never around. You're always at work, so you don't know anything that's going on and you don't care!" He turned to leave.

"You listen here!" Omar yelled, but it was in vain. Miles ran out of the waiting room, but once outside he remembered he needed a ride home. He decided to walk and brood, cursing his father, AJ, and anyone else he could think of. As he walked the five miles of city streets, he felt dejected and alone. Maybe everything really was his fault. Or maybe it was all the gangs, he decided. He was surrounded by them, and they seemed to be above the law.

Using some simple metrics, he measured each person he saw and labeled them.

If you wore your pants low, you were a gang banger.

If you wore a hoody, you were a gang banger.

If you wore your baseball hat backwards, you were a gang banger.

If you drove a car with others beside you, and it slowed down, you all were gang bangers.

Hatred gripped him, and the only thing that mattered to him was getting even with the BBB's. He thought about Kenny pestering him about wanting to go to the park and fly the plane, and he thought maybe he shouldn't have taken him up on it. Kenny and he were very close, and he had promised Kenny for a couple of weeks that he'd get a turn. Once he made the promise, he couldn't go back on it. Brothers don't do that, he thought. But he felt now that maybe he should have delayed it more. No, he decided, shaking his head. He realized that Kenny really was doing ok as a pilot, and he felt proud of his little brother for developing his skill.

Omar seeing the sliding doors close calmed down a bit. He tended to see things in black or white, with few gray areas in between. He looked at Bernestine, who had a much more nuanced look on life. He loved that about her, even when it annoyed him. Now he just needed to hear her thoughts; she had always had better answers to complex problems.

Bernestine standing over Kenny who was still unconscious held his hand while tears dripped from her cheek and on to his sheets. Just shook her head while looking deeply into Omar's eyes as she began to hum to calm her nerves.

"What are we to do?" he asked her softly. "I chose this neighborhood because it had a good community policing program. It was a little wild, but every neighborhood has its knuckleheads. Every neighborhood has its issues, but damn, what are we to do? Maybe we should just pack up and move further out to the suburbs like everyone else! Leave this damn place to the junkies, the drug lords, and the hookers, and let all those lazy asses just living off the state take over. I'm up to my eyes in all this crap," he seethed, with venom in his voice.

Bernestine soothed him with a gentle touch to his cheek. "Now you listen here, honey. No one's going to chase us away from our lovely home. We built something here, and we're not going to run away. You know that we got more than lazy folks living on welfare. There's more here than drug addicts and pimps. There are many young black professionals just like us, living here and doing fine. I'm proud of this place we call home. You just calm down. Everything's going to be ok," she said calmly.

Omar slumped and stared at the floor then out the window as rain splattered against the pane. "I know, honey, I know. I'm just frustrated, and seems like I can't do anything to make it right."

"Let's talk about this tonight after things settle down a bit," she continued, embracing Omar tightly. They brooded in silence, alone with their thoughts but together in spirit, as the minutes ticked by.

A young nurse came into the room gingerly rubbed Kenny's head, smiled then took his vitals. "He'll be fine" she said with a sympathetic voice as she turned and left.

Bernestine noticed that Kenny had a bit of a smile on his face, and she wondered what put that there. She didn't know that in his dreams, Kenny was still flying the airplane over the park, buzzing the tree tops and spinning into the sky.

After a bit, they talked one more time with the nurse and went home. They had no doubt that Miles would walk home. He had always used such treks for time to himself, and the local police knew he was Omar's kid, and they'd leave him alone. They took a route that they figured Miles might take, but they didn't see him.

Getting home from the hospital for the second time in one day, Bernestine slowed down as she and Omar approached the front porch. "Let's sit awhile before we go in," she said softly. She sat on the concrete porch, while Omar sat on the steps. "You remember when we used to come out here for coffee, chat with the neighbors and watch the kids grow up?" she asked. She had warm memories of those days, getting to know the neighbors and learning how things worked here. She nodded to herself at the memories.

"So much has changed. Even the place next door is different. It had all those hippy artisans , creating such wonderful things. We'd go to the Saturday market where we could get all our vegetables in the summer, and we even had the Goldsteins with their mom and pop store. They're all gone, and so many places been vacant now for years now. I wonder what they're going to do with this place if we move." She let the thought trail off.

Omar sighed heavily. "Don't know honey, but I do know realtors keep pestering us about selling. I bet as soon as we'd sell it, they'd tear everything down and build condos or something."

"Well, they can just wait. I'm in no hurry to move and make Kenny have to start at a new school. Miles, he's almost done and will be graduating in June. He'll be getting out of here on his own."

Omar wondered where this was going. It was probably going to come back to his ultimatum that he was already regretting.

"That boy better not be out late," he said irritably.

She looked at him. "He's just gathering his thoughts. He'll get home all right."

"He better," Omar said.

Bernestine continued. "I'm so proud of Miles," she sighed, looking deep into Omar's eyes and seeking confirmation.

Omar nodded. "He's a good kid. I know he and Kenny are just step-sons, and they don't have my name, but I love them just the same. I may not show it, but I do. I don't exactly know how Miles screwed up with his brother today, but it could have been worse."

Bernestine nodded. "It could have been a lot worse. I see it every day, gunshot wounds and drug ODs. They're kids out there suffering, and ours are finding their way. You've been a good father to them, and they know it. We'll see what Miles does when he graduates. Hopefully, he'll find something that will interest him and he can make some money. He's thinking he'll be a pilot, but he'll have to go to college for that."

Omar shook his head. "We got two salaries and we haven't had much luck saving up for college for those boys," he said wistfully. "If I could get a couple promotions at work, that would sure help," he said while standing up and stretching.

Bernestine stood up, too. "Miles brought home an application we need to talk about. It's called the High School to Flight School Program, but maybe tonight isn't the time to talk about it. We all had a long and trying day. Tomorrow will be better," she said hopefully. She gave Omar a long, affectionate hug as they both went inside.

Arriving at the hospital the next morning Bernestine and Omar walked cheerfully expecting to see Kenny sitting up in his bed watching television. Instead as they both pushed the curtain out of their way they stopped in horror. "What?" but before they could say another word.

"Mr. and Mrs. Watson, I presume? I'm doctor Snelling. You mind stepping out in the hallway, I'd like to talk to you" he requested as he pushed the curtain out of their way. "Don't be alarmed with all the tubes they're preventative."

Omar standing defensively just glared at the doctor. "What's wrong with my son?" he demanded.

"Early this morning it was reported during the shift that your son woke up and complained of being hot. His temperature had climbed to 102 and he began shaking. His wound was swelling so I was called in while we gave him antibiotics. I see no reason to be alarmed but we'll keep an eye one him" he said attempting to reassure them. "

Omar's cell phone went off so he excused himself while Bernestine walked quietly back into the room. Sitting down next to Kenny and lovingly running her fingers through his hair she began to cry. "I know you can hear me son. It's mama, I'm hear. I know you'll be ok" she said staring deeply at the monitors. She reflected on one of the last gestures she remembered when she was yelling at Kenny for not completing is chores. So irrelevant she thought as Omar's hand was felt on her shoulder brought her out of her private thoughts.

Bernestine attempted to get Miles to accompany her and Omar to see Kenny, but he always declined saying he couldn't see him that way. Little did they know Miles rode his bicycle to the hospital practically every day while they were at work. He sat at the side of the bed and cringed at the beeps and sounds of the medical equipment. This particular day he didn't even notice the nurse who had come in to check Kenny's vitals during her rounds and it startled him.

"Hi, I'm Tasha, his nurse. Would you please move over to the other side until I'm done here? I've seen you hear almost every day. He must be very special to you."

"Yeah, he's my younger brother and it's all my fault he's here. It should have been me and not him" he said in a soft voice. "Aw, why isn't he moving and what is all this stuff anyway?" he continued somberly.

"We're monitoring his breathing, giving him fluids so he doesn't get dehydrated, some nourishment and medicines to help with any infections."

"But why is he asleep every time I come here?

"We've sedated him so he'll remain still. We don't want him moving around until his wounds are all healed" she said while typing her notes in the bedside computer.

"Can he hear me?"

"I don't know but it's ok to talk to him. Sometimes it helps" she said with genuine smile as she turned and left.

As the curtain closed Miles looked down at Kenny as his lips quivered. "I'm sorry lit'l bro for what they've done to you. If I could take it all back I wouldn't have let you fly knowing AJ and his dawgs were in the park. They're always causing trouble. But believe me lit'l bro, they're gonna get what's coming to them. That I promise!" he continued with anger and a revengeful tone as his eyes glossed over.

CHAPTER 4: Off the Roof

A few weeks later, Miles while riding his bicycle through the neighborhood when he came upon some kids that were talking about what they had just seen. He pulled up in front of a thin young man dressed in baggy shorts and a worn hoodie, sporting an earring and bushy Afro. "What up, Ralphie? What ya doing?" Miles asked.

"Oh, nothing, you know. Hangin'. I was just explaining to these idiots about this club I belong to." Ralph grew animated and continued talking quickly, as he usually did. "It's a drone racing club across town I've been going to now for about three months. We meet every Thursday at different locations. It's pretty cool, too. Gonna race my drone tonight over at the ole empty K-mart building. They're setting it up now, so I have to go." He started moving away, as though he had much more important things to do.

Miles digested all this quietly and said nothing, watching Ralph go.

Ralph looked back and yelled back at Miles. "Hey bro, you should consider coming down and joining. It's fun!" he added, hoping to get a response. "And besides, one of the guys saw you flying those old-ass helicopters and planes a few weeks back in the park when Kenny got hurt and said you're one hell of a pilot. Anyway, think about it. By the way how's Kenny?"

"He's still in the hospital and I don't think he's doing good. I go every day but he's sleeping a lot. "

"Aw man I'm sorry to hear that" turning away not wanting to engage further in that disheartening moment. "Look, I gotta go"

Ralph quickly remarked, turned and hollered back. "Let me know if you're interested in checking us out."

Looking envious, Miles stared up into the sky. "Yeah, wish I could fly them, but my ole man said I can't fly helicopters or planes ever again because of what happened to Kenny. You know how that goes, Josh," he said to a short, stocky boy with long dreadlocks and a bit of a Jamaican vibe to him.

"So, what's your ole man gonna do, arrest you?" Josh mocked in a Bob Marley accent.

The other two boys let out some "Yah, mahn" asides, long and drawn out, mimicking Josh because they thought it sounded cool. Then everyone started to laugh aloud; they were a million miles away from the Caribbean, and they knew it. Even Miles joined in, although he felt somewhat embarrassed about being a policeman's son.

"You want to go down to the bike park and do some jumping with us, Miles?" Josh asked, with much less of an accent.

"Naw, I need to get on home and get my chores done before my ole man gets home and goes hard ass on me," he said while turning his bike around towards home.

"Give me a call when he arrests you and we'll take up collection to bail you out," Josh hollered while the group started to head to the bike park.

Sitting in his bedroom after dinner, Miles started Googling 'drone flying' on the web. He became enthralled by what he saw, watching videos of screaming machines banking and twisting as a heavy rock beat backed it all up. "It can't be that hard to fly a drone professionally," he said to himself, looking at videos and pictures. "But Officer Johnson said I can't fly no more, period" he uttered sarcastically.

Miles looked for a way out. "He said I couldn't fly airplanes and helicopters," he muttered, as he attempted to justify what he was thinking about doing. "Maybe I'll call Ralph and see what he has laying around that I can borrow. I can learn to fly it so my ole man doesn't find out."

Continuing to look on the computer, he was totally impressed with the many types and different functions of each device he saw. With the urge to fly, he switched screens from drone flying enthusiasts to the web site from HS to Flight School and he envisioned being accepted into the program. That would rock! He told himself. He spent the rest of the night in his chair, until he fell asleep with the screen lit up flying drones.

The next day, Ralph came by on his bike. "Hey, what's up Miles?" he asked, slamming on his brakes.

"Ah, nothing. I'm just wanting to do something but you know, nothing really to do. So, Ralph, I've been thinking about what you said the other day about me flying drones. Are they hard to fly? What's so different about drones than say helicopters?" he asked.

Ralph thought about that for a few seconds, like a feral cat instinctively tracking a rat he'd been tracking all day. "Well, I'll tell you. We haven't seen anything yet. They can not only fly, they can hover, or navigate without any input from the pilot. Try that with a helicopter and see how fast you crash. Or what about self-stabilizing or holding a GPS coordinate with a camera that shows real-time views? This shit is getting real, dude."

Miles leaned forward, excited. "Wow. Go onnnn," he said with obvious exaggeration.

"What about it locking on you so it can follow you or your car automatically? And best of all, it has an altimeter that informs you of its flying height. It can fight the strong winds, even tackle gusts up to thirty-five miles an hour, depending on what type of drone you have."

Miles nodded. Wind was a constant problem, especially with a lighter craft.

"And check this out," Ralph continued. "Say you're in the sky and your drone can avoid obstacles in its path and land automatically. Now, that's what drone flying is all about. Everything you know on steroids, man. I know you love your little 'copter, but things are moving so fast, and it's just so cool."

Miles shook his head. "That is so cool," he acknowledged.

"So, to get back to your question about what's so different about them. If you're not racing but just flying around they're pretty easy to fly. You've never flown one before? That's kind of crazy, where you been? I'm surprised we never hooked up to fly them, but I understand we both had things to do and besides you said your parents didn't support that idea."

"I don't know, I kind of like flying what I fly or at least I used to before I was grounded," Miles said defensively. "I'll think about it and maybe one day I'll try 'em," he added hopefully.

"You want to go down to the park? I have a couple micros and I'll show you how to fly 'em," Ralphie said, pulling one out of his back pack.

"Naw, I don't want my ole man to drive by and see me after I was ordered to stop flying," he cautioned, pretending it didn't count for flying drones.

Ralph put it back in his bag. "C'mon, it won't take long. You want to go up to your room and I can show you a few moves to get you started?"

With that, the boys dashed up the stairs. Ralph reached into his back pack and pulled out two quad micros. "These guys are my toys I play around with. They're small, but they pack a bit of sassy in them. Watch this," he said, as he turned on the drone and transmitter. Ralph held out his open hand, placed the drone on it and immediately flew it off around the small room. "I'll take it up towards the ceiling and WHAM-O I'll do a couple of flips then set it over there on your bed," he said with glee in his eyes.

Miles was stunned to see what that little drone could do. He wanted so desperately to attempt to fly it, but Ralph didn't offer so he remained quiet. Once again Ralph took off and circled the drone, flying up and around the fan that was on. He almost crashed it because of the turbulence but got it quickly under control, saying "These little daddies don't do well in the wind. Watch out for that."

Miles leaned forward. Was that his cue?

Ralph smiled. "Ok, you ready to fly?" He handed the transmitter to Miles, he reached out eagerly. "Hold on and don't start off yet.

Let me turn off the fan so you don't crash it right away. OK, increase the aileron throttle."

Miles did as he was told and immediately flew it into the closet door. It bounced off the door and fell on the floor. "Oh, man, I'm sorry. Hope I didn't break it," he said apologetically.

"It's ok, they're pretty sturdy. But this time, don't give it so much forward stick." Soon Miles was flying within his room, but still not very steady. He felt so cramped and restricted; it wasn't like the park at all.

"Let's charge the drone," Ralph said. "It'll only take about thirty minutes, ok? By the way, do you still go on the roof next door to hang out?"

"Yeah, I do sometimes because I can get away from everyone and its quiet up there," Miles admitted.

"OK, let's pack everything up and go on the roof. You need more room to fly."

"Are you sure? I don't feel that brave yet," Miles admitted. But his friend had the confidence of youth, so they made their way to the side porch. Miles grabbed ahold of the homemade bridge and slid it across from the missing railing slots to the roof of the vacant building. It took no time for them to get settled.

Ralph again grabbed the micro and sat it down on the roof. Immediately he launched it high into the sky until it almost disappeared. He then brought it back down out of sight, then back on the roof top where he did multiple flips. "I'll take it to the end of the building and bring it right back," he said excitedly, while staring at Miles' face with a grin. "Kind of cool, isn't it? So small, so quiet, and you can do a lot of things with it. Here you fly it now, but just remember small moves do a lot, ok?"

Taking the transmitter, Miles flew the drone only a few feet off the ground and made deliberate turns so as not to drop it over the edge of the building. With some encouragement, he started to get more altitude and made sharper turns. Smiling broadly, he said, "Man, with some practice, this could be fun, bro!" He stared at Ralph and took his eyes off the drone.

"Give it power quick!" Ralph commanded, as the drone dropped down out of sight. It rose to eye level but when Miles attempted to turn it back on the roof, he turned it the opposite direction and it immediately lost power as he let the stick go. Both boys ran to the edge and they could see it on the ground next to a tree. "Look bro, I need to get home anyway, so I'll get it on my way out. Oh, here's the other drone. You keep it with the transmitter and practice. The next time I see you, don't tell me you lost it into a tree or it flew off and you can't find it," he said with a grin. "By the way, here's the charger you'll need, ok?"

Miles was elated. "Thanks, Ralph I'll take good care of it," he assured his friend. They quickly crossed back over to the porch into Miles' bedroom.

Over the next few weeks, Miles was amazed how quickly he was able to control the micro, and he lost interest in flying helicopters and airplanes all together. He was a quick study because the controls for the micro were practically the same for his helicopters. He was able to extract top speed, trim his micro to obtain more precise movements. He took pleasure in getting the micro to hover and he learned to spin it around in any direction.

One time a bird flew by and the micro was soon in chase at full speed. Even though he quickly gave up, it was exhilarating to think he could basically fly like a bird. He could fly backwards at full speed, then turn the micro facing forward. While dropping the micro over to the roof's edge, it became a challenge to fly it down closer to the ground and then bring it back up to him.

One day when he saw Ralph riding his bicycle up the sidewalk, he quickly launched the micro. With a quick directional turn, he dove the drone to within a few feet of Ralph, then circled him a few times before recalling it up to the roof. Leaning over the roof he yelled down a quick "Hey!" and began to laugh aloud. "Check it out, bro, I've been practicing like you said. I love this little micro."

Ralph smiled. "Yeah, I can see. You up for some flying lessons? I'll be right up," he said, hopping off his bike and throwing the chain around the wheels. Entering the bedroom, he gave Miles a big, loud high five.

"You charged and ready to go?" Miles asked.

"No, but It'll only take about thirty minutes," Ralph replied.

"While we wait, I'll tell you what I've been doing." With that, Miles began his story of how he learned to use the transmitter, being able to fly the micro in any direction at full speed, take it out to its furthest direction, swoop down and climb. He explained how he could hover because he had been playing around with the trim nodes. The best part, he explained, was that he was able to dart in and out of the tallest tree and then bring it all back as if to scan himself.

"Nice, bro. Ok, you ready for some lessons? Here's what we're gonna do. I'll take the lead and you follow me and do what I do. Set your speed at the lowest setting and try to keep up, ok?"

Reluctantly, Miles set his drone at the slowest speed and away they flew. Soon they were flitting through the air, up, down, flipping, diving, in and out of the trees, quick stops, and more flips. They were synchronized tightly, hovering, spinning around and performing amazing stunts. Miles was pleased that he was able to keep up with Ralph, and he occasionally drew excited praise in the form of "Oh yeah!"

"Not bad, huh? Keeping up with you pretty good," Miles said with a wide smile, while chasing and doing everything that Ralph was executing.

"Yeah, well let's go all the way. Click to the faster mode. I'll leave your ass in the dust," Ralph said with confidence as he slammed the throttle forward.

The battle was on. When Ralph winked at Miles, he didn't see the maneuver that allowed Miles to catch up to him. Straining to put the micro through all the maneuvers he was aware of, he noticed how good Miles really was. No matter how he dove or climbed, Miles was right behind him. He flew off the rooftop, dove into the trees, skimmed the flat roof, blitzed around the chimney and still couldn't get away.

"Ok, I'm convinced. You really do know how to fly that micro!" Ralph acknowledged, as he brought the craft back to his hand. "You should really think about what I told you about, coming down to the club and see real drone racing. You'd like it, and the guys are pretty cool, too."

As Miles brought his micro back to his palm, it was just in the nick of time because it had lost all the power and dropped at his feet. As he bent down to pick it up, he noticed they were not alone. It was Kenny, who had been watching with amazement.

"What ya doing Miles?" he wondered, while walking across the bridge to the roof.

"None of your business," Miles replied, knowing they were caught red-handed at something that Miles was told not to do. "Now, don't you go telling Mom or Dad," he ordered in a tone that sounded like he was begging. "Ralph had just come by to show me his latest micro drones and gave me a chance to fly it quickly, right Ralph?"

"That's not what I saw" Kenny charged, knowing he had them where he wanted. "If you teach me how to fly your micro, I won't tell on you," he bargained confidently.

"The micros aren't mine, they're Ralph's, and I don't have any to teach you on," was all Miles could manage. He knew how weak it sounded.

"Hey bro, I didn't know Kenny was out of the hospital. When did he get out?"

"He's been out for a few days and supposed to be in his room resting" he replied.

As Ralph gathered up his micro, he thought for a minute. "Look Miles, you can keep this little guy and teach little bro how to fly it, and then you won't get in trouble if he squeals on you." With that he walked across the bridge and yelled back as he was climbing through the window. "Good luck and remember, don't wreck my micro."

With that, he disappeared, leaving Miles and Kenny on the roof. Miles knew that the last time they flew together, Kenny got stabbed, and Kenny's inability to fully control the craft, or else his natural inclination to show off, was actually the cause for Miles not being able to fly again.

He took a deep breath, then shook his head. "You listen here little bro. You know how mom and dad feel about me flying, and that goes double for you. Besides you just got out of the hospital. This is serious stuff, and if I teach you how to fly you can never, and I mean never, say anything, you understand? If you do we're both screwed."

"I promise, I won't say anything ever, I promise," was the earnest reply.

CHAPTER 5: First Race

Seemingly at every waking moment, Kenny pestered Miles into taking him up to the roof where he could learn to fly the micro. He had to change a couple of the blades after Kenny rammed the micro into the side of the roof, but nothing was so damaged that it couldn't be flown again. He enjoyed taking off and landing at different locations, and soon Miles set up some PVC hoops on the roof to fly through like a miniature obstacle course. They timed themselves and invented several different games to test each other; over time, Kenny even won a couple of heats, although Miles told him that he "let up" so he could win. In truth, Kenny was getting proficient.

The younger brother was never allowed to fly off the roof or to fly out of range. Kenny finally lost interest when his friends picked up the latest Artificial Intelligence game, Armageddon became the single thing he thought about. At first, Miles missed Kenny always pestering him, but he understood that a young boy needed friends besides his older brother.

Miles was no longer challenged flying the micro on the roof, and he became obsessed about taking Ralph up on his suggestion. He remembered so well that his Dad had prohibited him from flying helicopters and airplanes, but he rationalized a drone wasn't one of those things. Over and over in his mind he was being drawn closer to violating that order, but when he finally gave in to the temptation, he just grabbed the transmitter and micro and headed back out on the roof. It was there that he found his solitude, but he dreamed of something more, even if he didn't know what that was.

One Saturday while lying on his bed thinking about drones, Miles received a text from Ralph. "Big race 2nit @ 11 PM. Undrgrnd prkg gar 10th&Yamhill." Miles stared at the message and deciphered it. There was a big race tonight at the underground parking garage at 10th & Yamhill. Interesting.

He called up Ralph for more information. "Yeah, dude, this will be major," his friend gushed excitedly. "It's open because of a water main break that crosses at the entrance. They only work on weekdays, and so we're gonna do it tonight. It'll be our club against a cross town rival. The cones and hoops will get set up earlier and by the time we get there, we'll have probably a good hour before we have to scoot because we didn't get permission to be there. So, if you're in, hit me back and I'll swing by around ten or so. Out." Ralph hung up quickly, and Miles stared at the phone. Could be epic, he thought. He wrestled with his conscience a bit more, negotiated several chores from his mother to allow him to spend the night at Ralph's, then texted back "IN."

Just before reaching the underground parking garage, Ralph and Miles met up with three more of his friends who were also raring to go. Across the street four members of the rival club, FlyN Fast, showed up. They were tricked out, all wearing matching T-shirts sporting the phrase Got Speed. After eyeing each other warily, they greeted each other.

The competitors next darted into the garage and pedaled down to the lowest level. It was chosen because that would give them the advantage of getting away if caught, because there were three exits and the sound was more muffled from that level. As per custom, one person from each club met to discuss the race parameters. Ralph did the honors for his crew, and was soon in discussion with his counterpart. The rest of the racers parked their bikes and made the last-minute adjustments to the painted PVC gates.

Next, the two teams huddled up. Miles hung out with Ralph's team while they discussed tactics, positioning, and order. Ralph repeated his instructions to be on alert for the cops or security that might stumble on them while patrolling the garage. Winning the race was important; not getting busted was even more so.

Everyone who agreed to race set up their drones, and synced their head gear to make sure their cameras pointed slightly upward to give them a better heads-up view. They each settled on a radio frequency that was unique. The visiting team had someone use a heavy chalk line to mark the starting and finishing line. One from each team would do rock, paper, scissors to see who would do the countdown to start the race.

Miles couldn't totally believe he was actually going to observe this race. Ralph called him over and told him to wear his extra Lite Head goggles and he'd use his extra pair. The call was on. Everyone got one practice lap to ensure they knew where all the markers, tubes and rings were. Ralph was confident as ever, as he had flown against the FlyN Fast's before. "Hey, Miles I want you to stand or sit right here and no matter what happens stay put because any movement usually distracts the pilots and you don't want to get thrown out of the club before you get in, ok?"

Miles moved to his assigned spot and stared intently as the racers placed their drones behind the starting line. He mentally inspected each machine, recognizing some from web videos, and dying to interrogate their owners about the technical specs. He wanted to know more about why some chose the designs, colors, head gear, and transmitters they were using. He mentally filed away his questions, as he knew it would be better to ask after things settled down. Plus, he was keen to see who won; he picked out a couple that he thought would be contenders.

Seven drones were lined up ready to go when the starter began his countdown. "Remember five laps only and afterwards we'll compare notes over at Alley's Game Room and set up our next race." Miles looked around and noticed that while all the drones were lined up neatly, the actual racers were spread out. Some were halfway down the course, another was sitting on his bike seat and another had brought a miniature triple leg chair. "Ok here we go. Ten, nine, eight, seven, six, five, four, three, two, one. GO!"

Immediately all the drones went airborne and quickly geared down into racing speed. Looking at Ralph's drone through the head gear made Miles sway and duck and make disturbing sounds thinking Ralph was going to crash. Someone told him sternly to shut up, which he sheepishly did.

On lap one, everyone was spread out. Some were low to the ground, while others coasted midway up and a couple chose to cling to the ceiling. The turns were unbelievable, and after a lap Miles took off the goggles and watched with his own eyes. But they darted by so fast he didn't see much, so he quickly replaced the goggles and took a deep breath. Suddenly there was a groan from one of the contestants on the other team when his drone came too close to the concrete pillar and it crashed violently, sending pieces everywhere. Miles saw it all, and he was thrilled. This sport was for keeps!

The contestant walked over to Miles and they exchanged a somber fist bump. Miles saw he was Asian, maybe his own age, with long hair that swept across his forehead and a faint beard. He sighed. "I'm Lee," he said.

"Miles. Tough break."

"My bad," Lee said. "I was pushing too hard. Your boy Ralphie is on fire."

Miles smiled. "Yeah, he loves this." Motioning to the controller, Miles frowned. "So, got a spare?"

Lee nodded. "Yeah, but that was my best rig. I'll have to rebuild another one before the next event. Most drone pilots don't go RTF, but I do."

"RTF?"

"Ready to Fly. A full setup, ready out of the box. Most pilots like to get all the parts and build a Frankendrone just the way they like it, but I wreck so many I don't have time."

Miles frowned. "Sounds expensive."

Lee shrugged. "Trust fund." They both smiled.

In no time, the race was over, but not without controversy. There was a small dispute between the two clubs; one contestant said Ralph missed the loop and flew alongside of it. But when they crowded around a laptop to look at the video, it turned out to be some fine piloting, and no infraction.

The challenger, a young white teenager with wicked dark sideburns, backed down immediately. "Sorry, my bad. You're too good, Ralph!" he said heartily, and the tension evaporated. The boys set up their second batteries and prepped for another go, Miles had wandered up to the lookout point and came running down quickly.

"Bike cop!" he hissed, and in a frenzy, the teams packed up their belongings, grabbed the gates and mounted up. In seconds, they were gone, leaving no evidence save for some shattered shards from Lee's destroyed drone.

Chattering amongst themselves, the pilots rode out to the designated meeting place. Everyone was blabbering about the course, mentioning how easy it was and that there weren't enough barriers. Suddenly, the chattering stopped as it dawned on Ralph who was complaining the loudest about the easy course – Lee, who had been the first – and only – pilot to crash.

"Says the guy who trashed his drone," Ralph laughed.

Lee blushed. "Well, sometimes I crash on the first lap, so it must have been an easy course!" he joked.

The FlyN Fast team leader took a swig off of his soda and tapped Ralph on the shoulder. He was a tall, strapping kid with dreadlocks and an easy smile that set off his athletic build. "Ralphie, who's the quiet kid you're hanging out with? He hasn't said a word all night long."

Miles looked around. "Just trying to stay out of the way, that's all," he shrugged. "What an extreme sport," Miles said with enthusiasm. "You guys rule."

Ralph laughed. "Shawn, this is Miles. I invited him to see what we do. He's a damn good helicopter and airplane pilot, but it's time to put away those kid's toys and step up to the big leagues," Ralph laughed.

"He must be pretty rich to be flying those aircraft," Shawn said with a whistle.

Ralph shook his head. "Sorry, RCs. He flies RC's, not the real deal. I've been showing him some moves with micro drones, and he's thinking about joining our crew."

"Flying micros are nothing compared to flying these drones," Shawn declared. "At one point tonight, we were probably doing sixty miles per hour, and that's pretty good for a parking garage. But if you don't pay attention or take too many risks, you end up with a smoking pile of parts." Looking at his friend Lee, the group laughed out loud.

"It was just Lee's night. It happens to everyone sooner or later," Ralph said.

Shawn nodded, ready to wrap it up. "So, we're gonna meet at Clay's soccer field in two weeks from tonight. It's supposed to be a big sanctioned event with maybe a few heats, so ya better get to practicing cause the FlyN Fast's will definitely represent." There was some testosterone-fueled taunting and wild challenges after that, as one by one FlyN Fast team headed home.

Ralph's group stayed at Alley's Game Room so long they were told they had to leave as it was closing time. They agreed to welcome Miles into the club, and Ralph volunteered to get him squared away as to when they meet and what dues to pay. On the way home, Ralph told Miles some more good things about the club, and said he'd like being a member. "I know you're not much of a joiner, and you wonder what you're getting yourself into. But you can see the league is pretty diverse. We don't play that race crap here. You're judged by how you fly and not the way you look or speak, other than the teasing that sometimes get out of hand," Ralph said with a smile. "I get teased about my thick glasses and weight, and I guess being half Hispanic, but they know I can outfly most of them. A couple of Blacks joined us awhile back but quit out of the blue. That happened before I joined and I don't know what their reasons were."

Miles said nothing, letting it all sink in. "To each his own, I guess," he finally said.

"Yeah, I guess. You still wanna crash at my house?" Ralph asked.

"Nah, I'm ok," Miles said. "I'll just tell Mom you have to get up early."

Ralph shrugged. "OK, no problem. I'll catch you later. Practice your moves!" he said, and they slapped out an elaborate fist bump before splitting up.

CHAPTER 6: In All the Way

Ralph had a workbench in his basement where he tinkered with his toys, and the two boys were hunched over it a few days after the big race. Ralph was looking for a specific cable, and rooting through all of the gear so far had not produced the scarce part. He tossed down a rag and slumped back on his chair, defeated.

"I must have lost that cable," he muttered. "Oh, well. I'll find it as soon as I buy another one," he laughed.

Miles frowned. "This is one expensive hobby," he allowed. "Where do you get all your money?"

Ralph shrugged. "I do chores, and I have an allowance. Plus, I've been selling off some of my baseball cards. I can't seem to dump off Barry Bonds' rookie card, tho," he laughed.

They grinned. "Cuz he's a cheater," Miles said fiercely.

"Yeah, I didn't know that when I picked it up," he admitted. I wonder if there are any PEDs to make us better racers?" he laughed.

"Don't need 'em," Miles said.

"I heard one group is into Ritalin," Ralph snickered. "As if..."

They were silent for a moment, lost in pharmaceutical thoughts. Ralph broke the spell. "So now that you've seen us race, what do you think? You want to give it a try?" Ralph located a screwdriver and began to make some kind of adjustment on his racer.

Miles paused. "I dunno. I can't afford one of these things, and my ole man is pestering me about getting a job. Besides, I don't want him to catch me flying," he added.

"I've been talking with some of the guys, and they seem to like you, but don't let it go to your head. Seriously, they like everyone," Ralph bantered. "There is something that might help you get going. The guys were saying that some of them are going to upgrade their systems, and they are thinking about donating their old drones to the club for spare parts. So maybe there will be enough parts to build you one, if you're interested."

Miles nodded. "That sounds cool. Yeah, I'm in," Miles said. "I'm not too proud to take hand-me-downs."

After a moment, he continued. "Also, I've been thinking. Seems like no one ever wants to set up the courses for racing or take them down when it's all over. Everyone just wants to race. What if I volunteer to set up and take down the courses that we're assigned to? I could even scout out places for future races. That way I'm kind of doing my part, and maybe that'll help me pay for some of the dues, too."

"Sure," Ralph said. "The grunt work is never fun. Somebody has to do it."

Miles nodded. "I've got a couple of ideas that might work. I saw some cool courses on the web, too. But the recon is the hard part. I was wondering if you'd like to bike out with me tomorrow and do some surveillance?"

"So, what ya doing now?" Ralph blurted out. "If you got some time, let's get some air. I'm probably doing more harm than good on this thing anyway," he said, tossing down his screwdriver.

Riding down the street, they couldn't help but play follow the leader doing a few street tricks on their bikes. Their favorite maneuver was jumping the curb doing a 360 and immediately bragging about how smoothly and far out they landed. Ralph liked taking chances, and he liked lifting his bike and riding the front wheel, whereas Miles would lift his front wheel and ride the back in a conventional wheelie. Both would laugh at the other, but as they tired, they returned to the discussion about the fact that drone racing is just in its infancy.

Ralph spoke between pants. "Pretty soon we can race with other teams from all over the region. I'm guessing pretty soon there are gonna be big national and international races, too."

Miles liked that idea. "It's pretty clear that drone racing is gonna be big. You can tell from the videos that it's made for TV. There could be big prize money, trophies, sponsorships and all that stuff."

"Oh, yeah," Ralph agreed. "ESPN, the Olympics...sky's the limit."

Miles laughed. "Yeah another sport only people with money will get the opportunity."

Ralph maneuvered around a pothole and laughed. "So, you've noticed a lot of different equipment everyone is using, and you can tell who has the money because they have the most slicked out equipment you can buy. Just keep in mind the most important thing. You can't fly and keep up with others if your first-person view system is raggedy. Most beginners don't even realize that just because you have a camera you can't see where you're going at seventy miles an hour. You gotta get that tilt just right."

Miles agreed. "I read up and learned a lot. The camera also needs to have a high frame rate and a wide field of view so you can quickly see around turns. Let me see if I have the acronyms down. FPV is first-person view. FOV is Field of View. That right?"

Ralphie slowed down. "You got it. Oh, and the transmitter must be capable of running the firmware called Dust-Off. Everyone is getting this system, and like everything else, I'm sure there'll be something soon to replace it. Once we get your drone built, take it to a place like a soccer field where you can do some free styling. Don't use your goggles because the easiest way to test and tune your drone is to use line-of-sight. Once you get the hang of this then you can start using FPV."

"So how did you learn all this stuff?" Miles asked. "It's part technology, part acronyms, part vocabulary, and then you've got all the different language stuff. There's this surfer-dude part, where guys talk about 'gnarly' action, and some skateboard patter tossed in. How do you keep up?"

Ralph stopped at a stop sign and rested. "I dunno, just live it. Being around all this stuff all the time, you learn pretty fast, I guess."

Miles jetted off ahead and turned down an alley. After a short sprint, they stopped at an open field. "There's a soccer field over here I was thinking about. We could set up a course where we take over the entire field and use the goal post as the starting line. We could dart over the fence, turn around over there by the light post, go along side those trees. You see that tree with the huge V, that could be fun to fly through, and then re-enter the field over there and back to the start," Miles said with a grin. "It won't take many hoops either, maybe three or four."

Ralph nodded. "Not bad, bro. I can see you've been thinking about this for some time. By the way, the club may be getting our own air gates, then we won't have to use them ratty-ass PVC hoops, which are falling apart. They can be fun, but having to go through some real gates is even better especially the florescent lit ones."

Miles was deep in thought. "I may need to get a wagon to carry all that gear. Flags, streamers, cones, rope lighting, arrows, man." He paused and looked up with a grin. "I'm not complaining though," he pointed out with a laugh. "I asked for it, huh?"

"Yep, you begged," Ralph said, nudging him in the ribs. "Don't feel all jacked up about a lack-a-money. I was lucky. My Mom supports my drone racing because it'll keep me out of trouble. She'll do anything to keep me away from the gangs that are trying to take this whole damn place over. At least racing drones, it takes me out of this hell hole we live in and gets me across town," Ralph said with a disgusted look on his face.

Miles shrugged. "It's not so bad. Everybody got to be from somewhere."

They parked under the V-shaped tree and enjoyed some shade from the summer sun. Ralph slumped down with a heavy groan. "You asked me what I like when I race, so let me tell you. You've seen my Lite Head FPV goggles. They cost somewhere around $330 dollars or so. There's another pair called the Contender X4 that cost around the same."

"Damn, that's already serious coin," Miles brooded.

"Yep. My racing drone is an Angry Scooter 511 quadcopter with GPS. It's carbon fiber for weight savings, but also strong enough to withstand most of my crashes. I use brushless motors because they last longer. Cost about $600 or so. Mine is about 6 1/2 inches long and only weighs about two pounds. Originally it came in white, but I had my buddy Garcia spray it with a light coat of reflective material so it'll be seen in almost any condition when my LED lights are turned on."

"Tricked out!" Miles said approvingly. "Garcia? Dude that always smells like paint thinner?"

Ralph nodded. "The same. He's the one that used to do the fancy-ass tagging around the neighborhood, pissing off the cops, until someone noticed his paintings and got him off the street. After finishing community service, he started trick'n out rides, and now he's part owner of his own painting shop. He's a serious good artist, man. Serious. You dream it, he brings it to life."

"Tell me about your batteries," Miles said. "Ole Pops at the park said he used to fly planes with a special gas. Says he misses the smell of high-octane fumes in the morning."

"I'll bet he does. Crazy old coot. OK, so, something about my battery pack, I can fly for around ten minutes and that's better than most. But our races are over in five to six minutes. This machine will go around seventy-four miles per hour, which is bitchin' fast. For a big tournament, you'll need spare power packs. You got to pay attention to that power gauge at all times, man. I ran out of juice on a turn once and it wasn't pretty."

"What about the camera, that must be pretty spendy?"

Ralph nodded. "The camera has to have a very high image quality, because at that speed, you'd better be sure you can see where you're flying. They'll get out of your line of sight and you'll need that view. Believe it or not, I can fly her 1,000 meters."

"Meters? Talk American, you sissy," Miles jabbed.

"That's 3,281 feet in case you didn't know ya math, junky," Ralph countered. "Like I said, it has a GPS and has an automatic return to home when the battery is low. You already know about my Laid-Back transmitter. It has a 4x6 extra screen that I can use or wear my Fat Shark goggles."

Miles jumped up and peeled off, headed down a path through the trees. Ralph struggled to get up and follow. "Where are you going now?" he yelled. "What's over there?"

"There's a couple more places I want to show you," Miles said over his shoulder, darting along the crooked dirt trail. "On the other side of the trees, there's a big vacant field, next to K-Mart. The back of K-Mart has a huge parking lot."

They pulled up and marveled together. "Look at the trees, man, this would be a great course with all the paths, and we could even fly through those huge drainage pipes that haven't been installed yet," Miles added. "We could use the duck pond, its trees, light poles and building as a course. What ya think?"

"Yeah, cool bro, definitely possibilities." Ralph was smiling.

Over the next two weeks, Miles not only did his part but the team accepted him and helped him to build out his first racing drone. It was a "Frankenbeast" as Ralph called it, with mixed and matched cast-offs and quite a bit of glue, tape, and extra wires. It had different colors on each rotor, and the fuselage was beat up and cracked. But he loved it, and was proud of it, naming it "Sparrow."

Unfortunately, he didn't get much practice in, and his first race at the K-Mart track ended quickly when he over-corrected and crashed badly. He needed time to get used to the controls and the camera view, but he was forced to learn on the fly. He put all the pieces in a brown paper bag and got back to work at Ralph's work bench, eventually putting Sparrow back into action.

The next weekend was a big deal. Multiple teams were coming from all over the country to compete, and a few international contestants were on hand as well. When Ralph and Miles pulled up on their bikes, overloaded with heavy backpacks, they took it all in without a word. There were friends, fans, and family milling about, and a TV crew from the local station. There was a taco truck selling food, and hip-hop music blared from speakers.

The course was organized in a vacant manufacturing plant straight out of a video game, with massive concrete pillars, gaping holes where windows once sat, and tall, airy ceilings. No lookouts were needed - sponsors had rented the old building for a pittance, and all the proper permits were in place.

The course would be intricate, with multiple turns between the beams, through the loading docks, up a stairway and through multiple lighted air gates. Miles marveled at the assortment of prizes displayed on multiple tables for pilots and viewers to see as they strolled along.

"Man, I never realized that there could be so many different types of drones and goggles and gear," he said to Ralph as they parked. "Can you believe it? They have their own T-shirts, Ralph. This is happening!" Miles rubbed his hands in anticipation. His pulse was racing.

CHAPTER 7: The Finisher

Miles started humming the obnoxious theme music to *Pushing Mach 5* to calm his nerves. As he looked at his competitors, off to his right someone caught his attention. It was Katie Slauson, the skinny little white chick that had crushed Ralph on a sprint to the finish line more than once. He'd never raced against her, but he knew her name. She wore her usual Yankees baseball hat backwards, with baggy pants, and a T-shirt that read "Look now - you won't see me again."

He didn't realize he was staring until she turned her head and locked eyes with him. Her blue eyes were calm and cool, and he looked away, trying not to blush. He had assumed that he didn't like her because she seemed so brash and cocky, and she always brought a top-level drone. She also took great pride in beating the boys.

Now he didn't know what he thought about her. Her half-cracked smile meant she would have her 'A' game today. He knew she would be trouble on the course. Something occurred to him – maybe he secretly felt that she was kind of cute? Maybe he wished he had the courage to go up to her and talk?

Maybe he better get his head together, he reminded himself. She was cute in a skinny, geeky way, he decided, but she wasn't THAT cute.

An older white guy with cargo shorts and an "Official" orange jacket grabbed the mike, tapped it, and called everyone together. "Welcome to Super Drone Derby!" he shouted. "Are you ready to see some racing?"

The crowd responded with a group yell, and he grinned. "Special thanks to our sponsors, who make this all possible, and to everyone that's here – to the racers, the fans, and the officials. Let's get ready to rumble!" he shouted, and the crowd roared with approval.

"First, a few preliminary announcements. Keep in mind that this is a new sport, just in its infancy, and we want to grow the right way. No negative energy, no side bets, no smoke bombs, and no crashing into another drone on purpose," he laughed, and the crowd snickered, too. "Our ultimate goal to make drone racing part of the T-Games," he said hopefully, referring to the growing global league of eSports and drone racing. "What happens here today might lead to a positive future, or one that kills the sport. So, let's show the world what true sportsmanship looks like." There was lukewarm applause to that line; some in the crowd would be happier if the match were more like a gladiator event in ancient Rome.

He smiled and plowed forward anyway. "With that, here's how the event will run. Pilots, when you check in at the table to my right, you'll see the sign-in sheet. Once you sign your name you'll choose from the radio frequencies listed. Each person will be assigned their own frequency. There will be a sheet to identify which class you will be participating in. It will either be micro-maximum of 150 millimeters, the mini-up to 250 millimeters, or the open, up to 300 millimeters. All contestants must have video piloting capability. You must be able to take off and land vertically. Remember, safety first. If you crash, you must stay off the course until the race is over to retrieve your craft. It will be your responsibility to show up at the starting times with the proper class drone, so make sure you know your class. Lastly, because so many of you have come today for this first-time event, we've set up three identical courses, so pay attention to the loudspeaker and keep your eyes on the monitors. Don't show up at the wrong course and miss your heat, because you'll be disqualified. All right, let's get those craft in the air!" The crowd roared again.

Ralph nudged Miles, who was standing in line. "You ready for this?" Ralph inquired.

"Ready," Miles said. "It's game day!" They bumped fists and made identical explosion finishes.

Ralph was anxious. "Man, I'm not ready. I gotta make some final adjustments," he groaned. "I think I'm gonna use this one to get started to feel out the course. I'm wanting to compete in the open class but I'll feel better if I stay in the mini. See? I'm all flustered," he laughed.

Miles smiled. "Breathe, Ralph. Soak it in. This is cool."

Ralph shook his head. "I guess. I just don't want to embarrass myself, ya know? I see you brought Sparrow back to life."

"She's flyin' today. She's ready," Miles said evenly.

Ralph nodded. "I think if you choose to race the micro heat, you'll do better, but it's your choice. You can sign up for the mini and the micro and then change your mind if you do good with the micro, but if you're gonna do both you should hurry and sign up."

"Yep, that's my plan."

"OK. Gotta dash. Good luck bro. I'm being called for my first round."

"Yeah good luck to you, too," Miles nodded. He had reached the front of the line, and he hesitated while staring at the table.

"C'mon, man, get to it," a young Asian teen called to him coolly.

With that, Miles quickly signed up for the micro and the mini. He had been doing the practicing on the micro and felt confident with it, but his problem was the over correction and unfortunate consequences.

The first event was a blur. He didn't know anybody to his left or right, but he noticed they all seemed to have new, top drones that looked far superior to Sparrow's black tape and wiring. But when the countdown got them started, he felt really good. His mind moved to a place where everything else was obliterated except his focus. He could no longer smell food, hear music, or even feel himself breathe. Sparrow moved smoothly through the course, rocketing quickly to the front of the pack like a rabbit pursued by hounds. He deftly moved up, down, over, through...and today, his moves were precise and minor, rather than the big over-reactions he was prone to. Nobody could catch him, and he won easily. He didn't even hear the crowd, or even smile as his name was announced, he was so focused. He wanted to go again, right now!

He quickly switched out his battery with the spare, readying himself for the second heat. He took a long pull from a water bottle, loosened his fingers and shoulders, and within minutes, Sparrow was back in the air.

During this race, he wasn't able to move to the front so easily. He was able to stay up with the three leaders, but couldn't gain on them. He tried a couple of moves to slice off a corner or shorten a loop, but nothing was working. Suddenly, a drone that had been in front of him all race went crazy and careened out of control. It knocked out one of the other leaders in a spectacular crash, and almost took him out as well. In avoiding the disaster, he calmly flew up and over, and cleared the debris by a finger-width. On to the next gate, he smiled, as he realized he was closing in on the front-runner. He pushed the speed as much as he dared, and deftly slid in and out of problems while inching up. With half a lap to go, he slid in front, and won the heat by a car's length. The crowd cheered, and this time, he gave them a wave. Winning felt good!

He was beginning to like this course, he realized. He knew it by heart now, and could do it blind-folded if he had to. He took another long swig of water and realized he was very hungry, so he made his way over to the pilot's area and scarfed down sandwich and inhaled some chips.

Ralph appeared behind him and congratulated him. "I saw you won again," Ralph said excitedly. "Me, too!" he laughed.

"Nice," Miles smiled. "Keep going!"

Ralph nodded as he hurried to his next event. Miles moved to another race and got set up as well, then paused to look around.

His heart sunk as he saw Katie bent over, fiddling with her drone. "Well, my day is over," he muttered. Any confidence he had quickly evaporated.

Katie looked up at him and smiled, then pointed to the lettering on her shirt. Her eyes narrowed, but she said nothing.

Miles was frozen, but somewhere inside him, the competitive juices boiled over. "I can do this," he muttered. "She's just a girl," he added. His thumb moved across Sparrow's beat-up body and he lost even more confidence.

"Racers! Lay your drones at the starting line and prepare to race," a voice called out. "Turn on your goggles and check that no one has your frequency." Miles took a deep breath, glanced over at the other competitors, put on his FPV goggles and prepared to launch his drone.

Five, four, three, two one, and everyone flew off. His take off was a bit shaky, but he quickly got into the groove. He slid into his racing mode, where he projected his entire thought process into the drone and felt as though he was sitting in its tiny cockpit. He leaned into each corner and swayed back and forth on every straightaway. The race moved in slow motion for him, and he relaxed completely, almost trance-like. Out in the world, his drone was screaming through turns, slamming through gates, and roaring into the straightaways, but in his mind, it was perfectly silent.

With one lap to go, he was almost neck and neck with his blue-eyed nemesis. He was gaining on her steadily, focused on the back of her silver drone. He subconsciously boosted the speed and nudged forward with a slight lurch. No need to hold back now – second place was the same as last place when it came to beating Katie.

The hairpin turns, deep rises and quick drops were about to happen. Nearing the finish line, it was as though Katie's drone had dropped an anchor and he was gaining on her. For some reason, he flew right up to her with what seemed to be yards to the finish line, while her drone dropped speed and slid across the finish line under him, but slightly behind. It was ruled that he won that division, and Katie was second. The others behind them didn't matter, he realized, and with that, he seemed to wake up finally. The noise of the crowd crushed in, and he could smell food and hear music. His eyes darted around, unsure.

Katie sauntered out on the course and picked up her drone. She inspected it with an amused look, and asked quietly, "You ok, big boy?" She just shook her head, as though nothing had happened, and casually walked back to the finish line. Looking at Miles, she just nodded and smiled, momentarily acknowledging his victory, and then she walked away without a word.

Miles felt warm all over. That was a first, he thought. A girl didn't sneer at him!

Reporting to the winners table, Miles was so ecstatic he couldn't believe he had just won. He checked out the handsome silver trophy, which was about ten inches tall. The base plate was empty, with room for an engraving, and up top there was a tiny drone replica. He set it down and smiled and suddenly felt very, very tired.

Mechanically, he prepped for the next race, but never even made it past the first turn before he wiped out. Bam, and his day was done. He stayed and watched the rest of the races, filing away a few notes. Several of the racers were really skilled, and he wondered if he could even compete with them. When it was all said and done, his rival Katie won easily, when Ralph's drone crashed into the wall with one lap to go. Ralph groaned and looked over at Miles with a sheepish grin.

"Now who's over-correcting?" Miles laughed. They fist-bumped and took a seat, exhausted.

Katie walked over while they sat and stood over them, hands on fists, with the sun behind her. Her goggles were up on her head, and she had a bit of a dirt smudge on one cheek. Miles locked eyes with her again, and now something else stirred. She was a little plain, sure, but he liked that she was smart and skilled, he realized. He had never looked past her clothes and her attitude, but there with the sun blazing behind her, she was a racing goddess.

"You killed it, girl," he said, offering her a fist bump. She took it and their eyes met again.

"You're not so bad yourself. It's Miles, right?"

Miles smiled. "Yeah. And you're Katie."

"And we're both winners," she said.

Ralph groaned. "I had you, Katie. I was right on your tail."

Katie laughed easily. "Oh, I knew where you were. I figured you'd try too hard to beat me and splash that little craft of yours against a wall. Win or die tryin,' right?"

They all laughed. She waved and said, "Later, boys," and wandered over to the trophy table to inspect her prize. They watched her go, quiet.

"Man, I hate losing to her," Ralph said. "But she's just so fine with her moves."

"Yeah, real fine," Miles said dreamily. "I don't know how I beat her in the minis. I wonder if she let me win?" he muttered.

"Say what?"

"She dropped her speed real fast at the end, like she had a parachute behind her. She acted like she was adjusting something afterwards, but now I'm not so sure."

"Why would she do that? She never lets anyone beat her."

"Beats me. She's a girl. Nobody knows why they do what they do," Miles laughed.

"For freakin' sure, amigo," Ralph agreed. He let out a heavy sigh.

Miles stood up. "C'mon, you got one more chance," he said. "You can do it! Just remember that she likes to toy with you. She's tight on the right, but maybe you can sneak in over her left shoulder," Miles said thoughtfully. He grabbed a seat in the front row of the small bleachers, where he could watch all the pilots.

At the starting line, Katie was to the left of Ralph, along with four others further to the left. Miles could hear Ralph humming *Pushing Mach 5* just before the starter began his countdown. Five, four, three, two, one and they were off.

On lap one, Ralph was in the lead with everyone on his tail. Lap two was tighter, and Katie was edging ever so closely with him. Miles watched two drones wipe out right in front of the grandstand as they zoomed into view, and the spectators groaned. Now there were just four drones on the course, with one pulling up, sputtering on lap three. Three drones left, but it was a two-drone race, with Ralph and Katie going and back and forth, first one ahead, and then the other. On the final turn, it was neck and neck with Katie nudging ahead. She left her signature cushion, banking tightly to eat up the right turn, when Ralph saw his chance. Her left was wide open, and he pushed the throttle to the max and took his chance.

When they crossed the finish line it was a photo finish, and there was a flash as the race camera recorded the image. If this had been a late-night duel in the dark basement of an old building, the race would have been declared a tie. Katie looked to be holding on to her lead, but Ralph was closing ground fast. It took a minute for the officials to bring up the image and sort it out. Finally, they looked up. "Sorry, Katie. Ralph nipped you by a finger!"

Ralph jumped with delight and ran over to Miles, who was clapping and yelling with excitement. In the meantime, Katie just picked up her drone, looked back over her shoulder and nodded to both Ralph and Miles. It was as gracious as anyone could be in losing such a tough call, Miles decided. Classy, he thought.

After all the races were done and recorded, the announcer who had kicked off the day called everyone together. "How exciting was that, right? What a day! Now it's time for the presentations. We have three winners today but let me rephrase this. Everyone is a winner; however, trophies and goodies will only be given to the three pilots who won their final heat. So, let's get to it. Would Miles Watson come forward?

The crowd clapped appreciatively, and Miles smiled as he moved to the front. "Miles is the winner of the micro drone race," the announcer called out. "Congratulations, Miles. Here's your trophy, freshly engraved, and oh, by the way, your prize is in that wrapped box."

Miles picked up the box and shook it, curious.

"Will Katie Slauson please come up here?" As Katie moved to the front, the announcer continued. "This young lady won the mini drone class. Congratulations, and a job well done. Here is your trophy, and your prize is in the box over there." Katie ended up standing next to Miles, looking at her trophy and eyeing the wrapped box.

The announcer kept going. "Will Ralph Stenson please come forward? Ralph won the open class with some fine maneuvers, didn't he?" The crowd roared their approval, and Ralph beamed.

"Here is your trophy, young man, and of course your goodie box is over there," he said with a nod. "Everybody, please give these winners a big round of applause. And give yourselves a hand for your great support. Not bad for our first-ever tournament in the city, eh?" he asked, and the crowd applauded even louder.

"One more announcement before you go. We can't do this for each tournament, but we're trying to grow the sport, and to jump-start it, we wanted to give these three winners a special incentive to keep flying. So, their wins come with sponsorships, in which they will be flying their sponsors' equipment and wearing their jerseys. How about that! So please give them another round of applause." The crowd erupted one last time.

Miles looked at Ralph. "A sponsorship? That's just crazy!"

"To the victors go the spoils, I guess," Ralph said. He looked over and saw that Katie was already tearing apart the wrapping of her box.

She pulled away the last of the wrapping and gasped. Grinning broadly, she held aloft her prize – a brand new state of the art, recreational drone!

Miles was shocked. "The Felix 8 Quad," he muttered. He and Ralph soon were holding identical Felix 8 boxes with broad smiles.

Miles whistled. "I can't wait to get it home to see what'll do," he marveled. He looked to see what Katie was doing, but she had already tucked the box under her arm and made her way to through the crowd.

Ralph whooped with joy. "Oh, man, this is so awesome," he exclaimed. "Maybe I should take yours home so you don't risk being caught with it?" he joked.

Miles suddenly sobered up. "Whoa, you might be right. I don't know how I'm going to sneak it into the house without being caught. Even if I do, my obnoxious little brother will manage to find it, and he'll probably fly it into a tree behind my back."

Miles could almost hear his Dad yelling at him about flying. But he just shook his head at Ralph. "Nah, no, thanks," he smiled. "This baby is coming home with me," he said.

The house was empty when he got home, and he rushed upstairs and sat on his bed with the box on his lap. He opened it up and pulled out the user's manual, then shoved the box as far under his bed as he could. He added a few old toys, just in case his mom looked under there for lost socks, or other bits of clothing that didn't quite find their way into the dirty clothes hamper down the hall.

He leaned back on his bed and thumbed through the specifications. He scanned the words and read them, but it wasn't his voice in his head – it was the some high-dollar World Wrestling Federation announcer for a cheesy demolition derby at the county fair, making each factoid sound vitally important. "You get five high-definition cameras on board, with automatic take-off and landing, an un-erring automatic return to base, amazing HD video capability, and a hovering function that can't be beat," the voice yelled. His pulse was racing, and he alternated between putting the book down and savoring what he already learned, or reading more to maintain the spell. He opted to keep reading, this time in his own voice.

"The Felix-8 will stop in mid-flight to avoid obstacles, has automatic active tracking for any snoop flying, and has a battery life of 28 minutes," he read. "That's a far cry from the little five minutes I get now," he said with a quiet laugh.

"Man, I can't believe this," he continued. "It'll fly out to three miles at forty-five miles per hour. That is just crazy. I wonder how much it weighs?" he thought, scanning down the table of numbers.

"Oh, kind of heavy at seven pounds. OK, well, it's all muscle, no fat," he decided.

"One hour to charge the battery. Better get a spare," he said to himself.

Miles sat back in his chair and for a minute drifted off with all the data he had just read. Eyes shut, he talked quietly to himself. "This baby is made out of titanium and magnesium alloy, good for surviving all but the worst head-on crashes," he decided. He bolted back upright and resumed reading. "The Felix-8 comes with three flying modes: "trace" flying to follow behind the leader, "profile" flying to move alongside a designated wing man, and "spotlight" flying, with the camera focused on an object regardless of what the drone does." Miles whistled.

"My head hurts," he decided, and he got up to put the manual in his desk drawer.

The next day, Miles headed over to a park farther from his house and started learning the Felix-8. He set the Return Home function, flew the craft far away, the hit the button. The return home function automatically chose the best route to return, depending on environment conditions. It recorded its route as it flew, which allowed it to return along the same route back to base, which it could do even if the signal was lost.

He made several mental notes as he learned the new capabilities. When it took off, it recorded the view. Upon return, it checked the ground to ensure a safe landing. According to the documentation, if it found the return site unacceptable, it would hover and choose a new spot that was better.

Once the battery became dangerously low, the craft issued a warning and returned to base while it still had plenty of juice, so it must have been capable of some calculations based on speed, weight, flight, wind speed, and more, he guessed.

What really impressed was the 'Tap to fly' system, which allowed the pilot to tap the viewing screen and instruct the drone to lock on to that target. He didn't have a chance to try it out, as he ran out of battery way too soon.

Rather than return home immediately, he lay in the shade poring over the manual. One stat that stood out was the craft's ability to handle winds up to thirty-five miles per hour and still hold steady. His smaller, lighter drones would end up in the next neighborhood in a 35-mph wind. "I guess that additional weight is the difference," he said aloud. He rolled over and got into a more comfortable position, still reading. After another hour, he headed home and put his new flying partner back in the box, slid it under his bed, and set the battery in the charger. Then he kept reading at his desk.

Miles was like most tech-savvy kids, in that he was always keen on taking things apart to see what made them work. He'd been like that since early childhood, and he wasn't going to stop now. His closet and workbench were full of helicopter and airplane parts already, and the mess always drove his mother crazy. Still, she couldn't identify one part from another, and he had a project in mind.

He had to do something about the noise if he was going to be a ninja pilot. He couldn't get over the characteristic buzzing noise that his drone made, and he vowed to figure out a way to muffle the sounds. Over the next two days, he experimented with noise reduction, including buying a cheap blade balancer, scaled to the weight of the individual rotor blades. That didn't help, so he began sanding some of the blades and weighing them out to the exact same weight. Still no great impact.

He texted Ralph late that night – "Blades noisy-any cure?"

Ralph texted back immediately. "Try faster speed." He sent back a thumb's up and the next day, he was up early, bicycling to the far park. Nope, it didn't help. He tried slower speeds, but that didn't help much, either.

Next, he took apart his noise cancelling head sets and attempted to fit his engines with noise reduction shrouds between the blades and motor. His parents were at work, Kenny was off playing *Counterstrike*, so he worked from his roof top. With a few flights, he noticed the sound was still audible but he figured out how to keep the drone at a higher altitude to reduce the attention he surely would receive.

When the sun went down, he disconnected the night lights, as he would rather fly in the dark and not bring attention to his drone. After dinner, he went back to his room and called Ralph.

"I sanded the blades, added baffling, and now I'm just going up higher. It's getting better," he said.

Ralph laughed. "Yeah, how high up?"

"Five hundred feet?" Miles guessed.

"That's nothing!" Ralph said. "Someone had just recorded the highest altitude ever for a recreational drone. Get this - 12,467 feet!"

Miles was amazed. "No way!" he said slowly.

"Way," Ralph said. "These babies rock!"

"Well, I'll take your word for it," Miles replied. "No way I'm going to test that out. I'm afraid I'd never see her again."

"Her?" Ralph asked. "She got a name?"

"*The Finisher*," Miles said. "I removed the running lights. She's a phantom in the dark," he said proudly.

"I like it," Ralph admitted. "Let's fly tomorrow." They made their plans and called it a day.

CHAPTER 8: Witness to Murder

Summer was coming to an end, but until it did, Ralph and Miles met up each day at Ralph's workbench to tinker. One day while hanging out with his drone buddy, there was a discussion about America's continual involvement overseas with drones.

"It'll come from the sky. Death from above," Ralph said emphatically, pulling up a grainy video. "Predator drones firing Hellfire missiles. GPS-guided, hundred-pound payload – boom! No more bad guy."

Miles was intrigued. It wasn't warfare, it was a video game, and the humanity of the targeting was way above his pay grade. They had a rigged up a system to attach toy guns that fired foam balls from Ralph's Felix-8, and they set up toy plastic soldiers in a Lego fort in his back yard and blasted them on bombing runs.

After six straight successful operations, they retired to the basement and shared a can of Pepsi. "I wonder if there's a way to mount an actual gun on *The Finisher*," Miles asked.

Ralph shook his head. "Not on our little JV drones. The military is already doing it on their bad boys, but we can barely handle a ten-pound payload."

"You sure?" Miles asked. "We should test it out."

"OK, let's weigh out some of these metal pieces," he said, pulling together few cans of paint and a scale to weight them. They experimented to see just how much payload a Felix-8 could carry and still fly under control, keeping a written journal that had drawings and pictures of all his experiments.

They soon realized that they needed something even heavier. Miles figured out a way to fasten a brick that had three holes through it, by wiring it to the camera pod underneath the drone. It weighed six pounds, and the drone was still able to lift off. They added another one, and it was still able to jump into the air. They got one more on, and the drone was still able to leave the ground, although slowly. Ralph brought it back to earth, managing to lay the bricks down and land away from them.

"Wow, 18 pounds," Miles said.

"That's a lot," Ralph said. They just looked at each other.

Miles reached down and unstrapped the bricks from Ralph's drone and relaxed on the back porch.

It was Labor Day weekend, and Miles was left alone to more or less supervise Kenny while his parents enjoyed a rare trip out of town. Kenny was visiting his friends, figuring to play video games for every possible waking minute, so Miles planned to crash at Ralph's that night. Ralph's parents were used to Miles and liked him, and they were busy binge-watching a Ken Burns documentary series in the front room, so the boys were free to lean back and discuss their passion. However, the discussion eventually turned to what Ralph called "current events."

"Seems like every Friday or Saturday night, the gang-bangers are out raising hell now," he said angrily. "We got ambulances and fire trucks and cop cars roaring around town with their sirens blasting. Drives me crazy," he said.

Miles agreed. "Every so often you hear car tires screeching and even gun shots off in the distance," he said solemnly. "I started to worry about stray bullets, since those idiots will shoot at anything."

They grew silent, soaking in the evening now that the day had cooled off.

Miles sat up. "You know, I better head home. Tell your folks thanks, but I got to keep an eye on my little bro." With that, Miles biked home and was soon relaxing on his bed, watching drone videos on his tablet.

The night had quieted considerably, so it was easy to listen in on conversations from quite a distance especially with the window open. Miles overheard a commotion down the street that made him get up and look out the window. There were voices arguing, which was never good. People in the city were jammed together, suffering in the heat, and the pressure sometimes erupted out of nowhere. The voices got louder and madder. He wondered who it was.

With a smile, he pulled a fresh battery from the charger and prepped *The Finisher* for an evening flight. He launched the drone and turned on the video screen, making sure to hit the record button. He was curious about the argument he could still hear. "This could be interesting," he muttered.

Hovering high above the trees, he focused on a speeding car heading his way. What he saw shocked him to the core. The car stopped, and an individual jumped out and starting to argue with two others. All of a sudden, a gunshot pierced the night. "Damn!" he muttered.

The car sped off one way and the two individuals began running in the opposite direction. He decided to stay above them and see where they were running to. He followed them for about three blocks when he noticed that they stopped and threw something in a dumpster and continued to run away. He lost them in his excitement to keep the camera directed on them, because he forgot to use the tap and follow command. They disappeared under the trees.

Still shaken, he hit the return home button and the drone arrived back above the roof, hovering about five feet away from him, then landed. "You want a cookie or something?" he joked.

Fetching his drone, he immediately went back into his room and quickly removed the memory card. He stashed the drone in his closet under some clothes and slid the memory card into his laptop, wondering if he got a good video. If he turned it over to the cops, he'd have to explain the past few weeks, and his Dad would flay him. If he didn't speak up, he'd have a secret nagging at him, and a bad dude would be on the streets.

"Maybe it didn't record," he told himself. "Maybe the quality sucks," he added.

He groaned. "That would be worse, because I'd know, but I'd have no proof. Then what?"

He decided he better look. He found the file and dragged it over to his desktop, double-clicked, and it started. There it was in plain sight, in high-definition, clear as could be. The camera had a "low-lux" setting that practically could see in the dark. He saw the car come up the block turning off its headlights, then stop. One individual in a hoodie exited the back seat. The young man looked around, then walked up to the two young dudes arguing about something. One was yelling far more than the other, but the words were hard to hear. He seemed to want something.

The guy in the hoodie unzipped and opened it up, but the guy doing most of the yelling pulled out a gun from the front of his pants, yelled some kind of obscenity, and shot Mr. Hoodie once in the chest. The other person in the argument also had a gun out, pointed at the man bleeding on the ground, but he didn't shoot. They looked at each other, then took off running. The car sped off, too. Somewhere, a dog was barking.

Miles replayed the event, still not believing that he had just witnessed a murder; he assumed the man on the ground was dead. Fast forwarding and zooming in, he saw what he thought was AJ in the front passenger seat. He saw the two antagonists running, then slow down and toss something in the dumpster. At this point, he focused in as best he could, and even put the video in slow motion, but he couldn't recognize what they had tossed into it. Still, he could guess.

He heard thumping steps and just barely shut everything down when Kenny came running into the room.

"Hey, you know better than busting in here, little bro. You knock or you don't come in." Miles shouted, scolding his brother.

"I know, but did you hear that shooting down the street a little bit ago?" Kenny panted.

"No, sure didn't," Miles lied. His brother could usually tell when he wasn't being truthful, but this was important. "I was wearing my headphones," Miles said. "How do you know it was a gun shot?"

"I was over at Murray's playing *Armageddon* when we heard it, and his mom told us to stay down. She went to the window and peeked out, but she didn't see nothing. She was mad; she said it wasn't the first time, either. Her brother that was visiting walked me home, because he didn't want me out at night by myself, so that's all I know."

"Wow! Did you see a body?"

"No," he admitted.

"Well, there you go. Probably nothing. Get on to bed."

Kenny let it go. "I'm going to stay up and watch TV," he announced.

Miles sat there wondering what to do. He finally yawned and set his alarm for early in the morning.

When the alarm went off at 3:30 AM, it startled him and he jumped out of bed, still clothed. He stood up, then almost fell back on the bed as the blood rushed from his head. He sighed, regained his balance and decided to leave.

The last thing he wanted to do was wake his brother. He sneaked out to the balcony and lowered himself to the ground like he had done so often. This was his escape route when he, Ralph and others took midnight rides or, lately, midnight drone races. Once on the ground, he had to open the gate to where his bicycle was parked, unlock it, and walk outwards toward the sidewalk for his getaway.

He forgot to stow the lock, and it rattled and made quite a racket when it got caught up in the chain and fender. Halting in his tracks, he pulled it free, and then mounted up, pedaling away.

He was now wide awake, and the three blocks zipped past. He was totally aware of his surroundings, and identified each and every unexpected noise. A faint dog barking a half-block away startled him, but he knew it was Roscoe, a lazy golden retriever who just wanted to chase a ball.

Two cars zoomed past, but they didn't slow down or pay any attention to his silhouette. Continuing on, he approached the dumpster, but kept going as though he wasn't interested in it. He nonchalantly rode right by and gingerly came to a halt about 50 yards away. He pulled out his cell phone and pushed a few buttons around, smiling as though he were actually engaged, and then stuffed the phone into his backpack.

"OK, let's do this," he muttered. He turned around and rode back to the dumpster, stopping in front of it this time. Looking around the best he could in the dim light, he felt it was safe. He slid off his seat and stood there, motionless for what seemed like an eternity. Then, with the stealth of a cat, he slowly opened the lid and his ninja façade crumbled as the lid creaked something terrible. He almost let it slam back down when the stench from inside his nostrils. He felt his stomach heave. Gak! He started breathing through his mouth, while kicking himself for getting involved in this maneuver.

Cautiously, he placed his hand inside but didn't find anything right away. He set the lid back down carefully, but it made more noise that made him flinch. He retrieved his cell phone and flicked on the flashlight, then picked up the lid with one hand and looked inside. The smell was horrible – a mixture of rotten food, old slime, stale beer, and maybe something like a dead cat. He almost retched, but caught it in time.

He couldn't see anything interesting, and he knew what that meant. He put his phone in his teeth and carefully pushed the lid of the dumpster up and over, making far too much noise. Now he could climb in, so he reluctantly boosted himself up and over the edge.

His feet weren't stable, and he didn't want to touch the sides of the steel. He switched on his flashlight and poked around in the dark corners where even worse smells came at him waves. When it was too much, he stuck his head out for fresh air, and then checked around to see if anyone was watching. He almost wished he would have an excuse to call it off, but no such luck.

He pushed around an old tricycle, then a half-opened bag of garbage that was squishy and made his stomach heave again. He got down on his knees, reaching under some cardboard, and he moved something hard that clattered menacingly against the steel. He reached farther, head up to try to get fresh air, and his hand grabbed something that was cold, slick and totally unfamiliar to him. He pulled his prize from the shadows and in the faint light from the street lamp, he realized that it was a gun. Bingo!

Miles jumped quickly out of the dumpster, trying to maintain his stealth mode but very happy to be done. He put gun and his phone in his backpack, then put the dumpster lid back in place, again with way too much noise. He kept breathing from his mouth, sure he had something disgusting on his shoes, looked around, and jumped on his bike, making his escape.

In minutes he was back on his bed, out of breath, staring at the weapon he had retrieved. It was actually a pretty decent gun, he decided; it might even be something his brother would use in the shooter games he enjoyed. It had no laser sighting, no super-fancy extended clip, and it was kind of beat up. Plus, it had a chunk of garbage slime on the handle, and it smelled. But it looked bad-ass, menacing and potent. He wasn't sure what caliber or make it was. Shrugging, he wrapped it in a shirt and quickly placed it under his bed. He sat there in the early morning darkness and then lay back on the bed, hands behind his head, trying to settle his racing pulse.

Eventually he fell asleep, but soon the sun's bright rays alerted him that a new day was starting without him. He reluctantly got up, went into the bathroom and took care of business, making sure to wash his hands and face and checking himself for splotches of garbage slime. He brushed his teeth, and looked at himself in the mirror. What was he doing? He shook his head in doubt.

Back in his room, he retrieved the gun and took a picture of it with his cell phone to help with a web search. When he discovered that he had an AR-15 pistol, he just sat and stared at the ceiling. It was twenty-six inches long, with a seven-inch suppressor and a magazine. Reading more about the technical specs, he learned how to ensure the safety was on, how to disengage the clip, and empty the chamber. Pointing the pistol out his window like he'd seen in the movies, he suddenly became frightened and quickly put it back under his bed. Hearing someone outside his room, he quickly switched the computer screen to the HS to Flight School screen, just as his brother knocked on the door.

Miles moved a few things around. "Yeah, c'mon in," he said pleasantly.

Kenny looked around at the mess on the floor. "Dude, you better clean this up. Mom and Dad are back in a few hours."

CHAPTER 9: Bump Fire

At the next club meeting, everyone was talking about the shooting. Miles learned that it was, indeed suspected that gang bangers had killed a rival gang member selling drugs on the wrong turf. They discussed what they knew. The police had increased their stop-and-frisk of known gang members, and their presence was beefed up - especially in areas where known gang shootings had occurred.

Ralph snorted. "It's getting crazy out there. Every time you turn on the TV, there's been another shooting."

There were nods, and the mood quieted.

Ralph had a thought. "Let's load up these drones with guns and drive every gang member out of town!" he said quietly.

Everyone laughed, including Miles. But the idea did intrigue him. He thought to himself about looking into the remote triggering capability of drones, and wondered if his new gun could be attached to a Felix-8.

Back home, Miles pulled out his Felix 8 Quad spec sheet, sat on his bed, and read it for the umpteenth time. He decided to do some math in his book. It was on his workbench and thought about what the guys were saying about drones and guns. He reviewed his payload experiment notes and knew his drone could lift eighteen pounds more or less effectively, without losing too much propulsion or altitude.

After bringing in the bathroom scale, he made a table in his book, in a simple code. "A-1" was the pistol, which he weighed out to about 5.5 pounds. He weighed one 5.56x45 bullet from the clip at 12 grams, or about 0.423 ounces. He noted the weight as "B-1" in his notes, and he emptied what was left of the clip and weighed that, too. He wrote down "C-1" as about eight ounces.

His parents had gone to bed for the night, so he surreptitiously performed a quick experiment. He strapped his AR-15 pistol to the underbelly of his Night Hawk after removing the camera, and flew it around the rooftop, diving in and out of some trees below to test its stability. It seemed fine, and he brought it back down and returned to his room to do more research.

He already had a system for flying Sparrow as a foam-ball shooter. But how to transfer that technology to his transmitter and Felix 8? He scanned the web for several minutes and found what he was looking for – a trigger mechanism that could mechanically pull the pistol's trigger and shoot one bullet at a time.

"One at a time?" he complained quietly to himself. "That's not going to stop AJ's crew. How did those crazy-ass white boys shoot up schools like Sandy Hook?" he asked himself, referring to the massacre of school kids in Connecticut he'd read about.

He kept searching the web, trying different combos to come up with a better triggering system. He'd never been into guns before, so he didn't know the lingo. Then he remembered the Las Vegas shootings a few years back.

There was a system that permitted the gun to shoot as rapidly as needed by only pulling the trigger once. It was called the slide fire, and some called it bump fire, or a bump fire stock, or bump stock. Miles read aloud, slowly. "The slide fire takes advantage of the recoil from a shot, allowing the trigger to travel backward enough to reset before being pulled back forward onto the trigger for continuous fire."

"Damn," he said quietly, looking around to make sure nobody was watching. After some more searching, he found some specs for a plastic slide stock that weighed 8 ounces. He made a note for "SS-1" in his table and smiled.

"A homemade machine gun," Miles said, then frowned. "But a noisy one. Gotta make it quiet."

After more searching, he found what he was looking for. "When guns fire, they produce superheated and pressurized gasses. When the gasses escape into the open, the dramatic change in environment causes the loud sound of a gun blast. Suppressors, or silencers, work by making the transition more gradual for the gasses." He nodded and kept scrolling, learning more. He made another entry in his table; "Si-1 – 10 ounces."

"Might as well keep going," he said quietly. "A tiny little clip isn't going to scare AJ," he muttered. Sure enough, there was a solution – high-capacity magazines holding up to 100 rounds. Another entry – "MAG-1 – 12 ounces."

He did the math on 100 bullets and found they could weigh about 2.5 pounds of bullet weight alone. But he was still far under the weight of three bricks, so he felt like the plan was on the right track.

As for costs, he was dubious. He could purchase a suppressor, the slide stock, a magazine, and ammo for about $1200, which he knew was out of the question. And he wasn't going to be able to buy ammo anyway – he was too young.

Outside, a dog barked, and Miles emptied his browser history and put the system to sleep. He looked outside and was lost in thought. Then he saw a familiar car prowling the alley a block over. It was the same car.

"I bet I know where you're going," he smiled. He couldn't see the dumpster without launching his drone, and he didn't want to risk it. He listened as the car seemed to pause, and he thought he heard a dumpster lid bang. He smiled. "Sorry, fellas. You're going to smell like the garbage you are."

Soon enough, he heard the car speed away, seemingly in anger. It occurred to him that it would be nice to track the car around town, and he knew just what he needed. A micro GPS magnetic car finder tracking system would do the trick. Ralph had one on his workbench he might be able to borrow, but how to attach it? He felt he could construct a delivery system by using his micro foam ball drone. He yawned and turned in for the night, dreaming of drones and surveillance.

The next morning, he bicycled over to Ralph's house and borrowed his GPS tracker. It was a coin sized magnetic device he attached to his RC airplanes and drones while learning to fly before technology changes. It had a rechargeable lithium polymer battery with a four-mile tracking radius he could pull up on his computer. Ralph was headed to his grandparents' house, so he just tossed the tracker to Miles saying don't lose it. Miles placed it in his zippered pocked, zoomed home and went upstairs. His parents were at work, and Kenny was gone again, so he set up on his workbench and played around with a newly purchased powerful micro.

He sent the micro down to the street and tried attaching the GPS tracker to a parked car, but it didn't work right. The delivery arm wasn't long enough to secure the device and the blades kept hitting the intended target. So back to the work bench he went. He constructed a different system using electro-magnets, with a small electrical current that could engage easily. The test was successful - once he flew the drone to within a few inches of his target, he could remotely extend the arms and the tracker would be drawn into the vehicle. He would deliver a command from the transmitter that turned off the electrical switch, and the tracker would remain alone on the vehicle.

With enough practice, he was ready to go live. Around midnight that night, he sent up the Felix-8 to scout the neighborhood and spot the expected vehicle. It was pretty easy to find, about a half-mile away, with music blaring at the Quickee Mart. For phase two, he slipped down to the street with his backpack and pedaled off. He came up behind the convenience store, ducked in behind the dumpsters, and then moved to an angle where he could actually see into the store.

Sure enough, there were two arrogant homies walking up and down the aisles while the Korean cashier eyed them. They were lingering over Slim-Jims and Fritos, then trying to decide what beer to buy. They were in no hurry.

Miles launched his micro slowly towards the vehicle. With expert flying, he approached stealthily. Hovering ever so close, he slowly rose to roof level and tucked the chip almost in plain eye sight, but it was small enough not to be noticed.

He checked on the homies, who were now at the checkout, bantering with each other and probably threatening to not pay for their Scoobie snacks. Miles retracted the arms and launched skyward into the dark with a faint buzzing. He sent it too high and almost lost it, but the 'Return to Home' button saved him again.

Suddenly a bright light bathed the parking area, as a police 'ghetto bird' hit the store with its 1,000,000-candle beam shining downward. But the craft zipped back to him, hovered, and settled in his hand, and he stuffed her into his backpack and raced home.

Once upstairs, he immediately logged on to his computer and began to track the vehicle with the latest satellite mapping software. It went to a house he knew and stayed put, so he turned in. Over the next three nights, he tracked the car as it trolled the neighborhood, always settling at the same address for long stretches. Another plan began to form in his head.

The next night, he flipped on the tracker and noted that the power was getting low. He slithered down to his bike and pedaled over to the party house, taking alleys and dark stretches to reach it. There was the car, parked sloppily on the street, and music pierced the night. He heard the base from a popular rap song booming a block away, so he slowed down.

The house itself was a two-story affair that had seen better days and could use a coat of paint. The landscaping had gone native, and there was junk all over the yard. The police had been called to that location numerous times because of the noise, but the homies would turn down the volume until they left, then put the word out that the next neighbor that turned them in would have serious consequences. Now they acted like they were immune to any nuisance laws.

Miles decided to take a gamble, thinking they might have some of the accessories he needed for his plan. He just had to break into their car was all.

"Man, to catch a criminal, you got to think like a criminal," he told himself. So, he snuck up to the car, checking to see if his GPS was still attached. Seeing it, he pulled it off and placed it in his pocket. Looking down at the door locks, he discovered the driver's side was unlocked. Cracking the door open, the dome light came on, and that scared him so much he almost fell backwards.

Thinking quickly, he reached blindly until he found the door light switch. Before he pushed it, in his eyes caught the trunk latch. Quickly, he pulled it and the trunk cracked open with what seemed like a very loud noise. He then pulled his arm out and away from the door, and closed it ever so quietly. So far, so good.

He moved to the back of the car, staying in the shadows. He knew if he were caught, there was no way to lie his way out of it, and no way to run away fast enough to escape. But he was so close. He knew that once he opened the trunk far enough, a light would also turn on, so he would only have one try.

With all of his ninja stealth, he placed his body in a squatting position and scanned the house and the immediate area. Still quiet. He opened the trunk to eye level, and when the light came on he quickly surveyed the trunk and saw a rectangular box with the words 200 cartridges 223 NATO 5.6 written in plain sight. Next to it was a crumpled army-style duffel bag.

With one hand, he attempted to lift the ammo box, but he had no idea it weighed so much. He tried to use both hands, but that made the trunk drop on his head with a light thud. As he struggled to lift the box out of the trunk, it clanked against the bumper. But it was now or never, and he quickly placed it on the ground. Then he reached back in and grabbed the duffel bag, which was heavier than he thought it would be, and he banged his head again. He got the bag out, put the ammo box in quickly, closed the trunk, and moved the bag under his arm. Quickly he scanned the area again and then walked briskly to his bicycle. It was very difficult to balance the duffle bag that had no straps on his lap and peddle as fast as he could, but he soon had everything back to his room. When he opened the bag, he found that it was full of gear. They were accessory pieces that he instantly recognized as the very parts he needed – three silencers, two bump stocks, three assorted barrels, loaded clips of various sizes, and even a mini-tripod. Jackpot! He lay back on the bed, chest heaving, with a big smile on his face.

The biggest challenge remaining was rigging the system to dangle from the drone and fitting in the firing system, but he had enough parts to put all of that together quickly. Summer was coming to an end, and he would soon be swamped for time with classes and homework, entrance exams, and all of that time-wasting junk. Classes had started but weren't serious yet, so he got extra busy late the next night, and by Saturday, he was ready for a field test.

Early in the morning, he folded the drone down, and stuffed it into an old army duffle bag. He added the newly configured AR-15, with its bump stock and ammo drum, added some dirty clothes to the bag to protect his prize. He left some clothes to hang out just a little bit in clear sight, so as to give the impression he was on his way to the laundromat.

Cautiously, he pedaled his way toward the forest north of town, until he found a clearing with trash, old tires, and bullet casings in all sizes scattered everywhere. He checked to make sure no one was in view, then he assembled his drone and staked out some old worn-out wooden crates as targets.

He turned on the video, launched his drone skyward, set the altitude holder, slowly turned the barrel and pushed the remote button. The gun fired once, then continued with rapid fire, emptying the clip. Several birds took off, complaining in unison and scattering to avoid the noise. The drone jumped and twitched as the bullets spit out, recoiling furiously, which scared him to the point he almost dropped the transmitter. He realized that he had forgotten to lift his finger from the trigger switch, so he had just used up a lot of his bullet inventory.

He also realized that even muffled, the sound surprised him. The suppressor worked well, but it didn't completely eliminate all noise. There was still a distinct, tiny pop each time the trigger fired off another round.

Miles quickly commanded the drone to the ground, where he approached cautiously, as though it would possibly shoot him. He replaced the big magazine with a smaller, 10-bullet clip, and sent the craft back into the sky. This time he took the drone high above the trees, then brought it in at a relative high speed as it approached the target area. He zoomed in the screen on what he wanted to shoot, and with a remote pull of the trigger he emptied the clip. One or two bullets scored, but the rest just sprayed the dirt. But that was as much as he wanted to practice for the day; there was a long road home that would take at least an hour. He packed everything up and sped off, looking forward to reviewing his video.

What Miles didn't know was that he was not alone. Another teenager had watched him from up on the hill where kids jumped their bikes on trails and obstacles. Little did Miles know that their paths would cross again.

CHAPTER 10: Full Disclosure

That afternoon, Miles contacted his buddy Ralph with a coy invitation. "Bro, got news. Swing by," Miles texted, and Ralph soon replied "Will do."

Miles was so excited that he met Ralph on the front porch. Without saying a word, Miles turned and hurriedly ran up the stairs, with Ralph in tow.

"Take a seat. I gotta lock my door, 'cuz I don't want anyone coming in on us," he said mysteriously, which kind of freaked Ralph out.

"What's wrong with you?" Ralph uttered suspiciously, while looking around the room.

"Remember a couple of weeks ago we all were discussing the future of what drones could do, and everyone was fantasizing. Since then, I've been experimenting with my drone. I want to show you something, but I want you to promise me this is between you and me, and no matter what, you won't say a word to anybody. You promise?"

"Come on bro, it's me, Ralph, you can depend on me," he responded.

"No, seriously, I need you to promise me," Miles demanded.

"Ok, then I promise."

"Cool." Miles popped in his SD card on his laptop and started at the beginning. "I can't believe what I'm about to show you. Heck, I can't believe what I've done. I wanted to see how the Felix-8 was made, so I went online and was able to find the schematics. I started taking it apart one day, and before I noticed, I had disconnected the running lights. I thought I broke it but I didn't," he added.

Ralph wasn't impressed yet. "OK, so?"

"It made me think about stealth mode. I did some experimenting with rotors and the motors to reduce the humming sound. It still makes noise, but a bit softer."

Ralph wasn't feeling it. "You mean you brought me over here just to see this? Because if you did, all I have to say is so what? You took a couple of drones apart and modified them, ok, now what?" he shrugging his shoulders.

"Naw, that's not all, what I said was just to give you some background for what I'll show you now." Miles fired up the video of the shooting he had recorded.

Ralph leaned in, speechless. He saw the entire crime, and just looked at Miles. "WTF?" was all he could say.

"Now you see what all this is about. Yeah, I was flying around in stealth mode and I recorded a video of a senseless murder. And that's not all."

Ralph was dumbstruck. He just kept shaking his head.

"Move your legs over to the other side of the bed," Miles commanded. "I have something else to show you." Ralph did so, nervously.

Miles reached down under the bed and pulled out the AR-15 pistol, with all its new hardware. Ralph lost it. "Dude!" he almost shouted, then he put his hand over his mouth.

"Yeah, I watched them ditch it, and I figured I'd go get it so they couldn't shoot anyone else with it."

Ralph stood up, silent. So, Miles pulled up another video, of him shooting up the wooden crates.

Ralph just groaned. "Oh, man, what did you do to *The Finisher*? Now she's an outlaw!"

"Damn straight," Miles said fiercely. "I'm gonna get even with AJ and his gang bangers for what they did to Kenny. I'm gonna deal with these guys on their own terms. And no one will ever know because it'll come from the sky, when they least expect it," he said evenly.

"Dude, you can't just shoot them. You become just like them," Ralph said. "You're better than that."

"I'm not like them at all, Miles replied." But you know the rules. Come at me with a knife, I come at you with a gun. I know where they hang out. I took video of them drinking and smoking weed and acting like idiots. I got it all on film. AJ maybe heard me and looked up, but I was able to fly away into the darkness and hit the return to home button. They'll be another time, that I promise." He started pushing all his gear back under the bed, and felt better once it was safely stowed away.

"Man, video I get. You can record their crimes and tip off the cops. But guns? Are you freakin' nuts?"

"They started it."

"The hell? You gotta stop right now and turn this all over to your ole man. You know you can get in a lot of trouble and wind up in jail over this. Are you crazy? You've lost your mind! You'll get caught and maybe killed by those asses."

"They gotta pay," Miles said. "I got the tools and I got the talent." He shut down the video and closed the lid on his laptop with a thud.

Ralph wasn't having it. "What makes you any better than them guys if you shoot them? All they do is take advantage of others, the killing, the robbing, and for what? If I knew you were gonna be into guns, I would have never gotten you into flying drones!" he scolded, almost out of control. "This is not what drones are for, dammit! If this is what you're all about, you won't have to worry about me. I can't be part of this! You're on your own, man, 'cause I'm not gonna mess up my life for your revenge," he said angrily.

Miles hadn't expected this. "Man, we shoot bad guys every day in the War on Terror. How is this different? They're terrorizing my 'hood."

Ralph just shook his head from side to side. "Yeah, that's true," Ralph admitted. He calmed a bit, and even sat back down. "There's been some bad-looking dudes with tats hanging around outside the club, watching what we do and talking about starting up their own posse. They tried to get us to help, even offered money and the newest gear. At least that's what they said."

"There goes the neighborhood, again," Miles said coldly. "I say bust some caps at 'em and scare 'em off."

"Dude, listen to yourself. Get over it. You're starting to sound like your Dad."

Miles finally smiled. "That's cold," he laughed.

Ralph waved him off. "Don't I know it." He got up to leave just as Kenny showed up at the door. "Hey guys, what ya doing?" Kenny asked, attempting to push past Ralph. "Mom sent me to tell you dinner is ready, and to bring yourself downstairs. And oh, dad's home as well and he's not happy about something," he continued. Miles looked around; everything was safely stowed away. So, the three of them went down, and he waved off Ralph and sat down to dinner.

Dinnertime was like many other nights, mostly small talk, with no one really wanting to discuss the day's activities as everyone was tired.

Omar sat poised, ready to pounce. "So, Miles how's the job hunting coming along? Have you found anything?" he started off caustically.

Thankfully, the universe chose that moment to awaken Omar's cell phone, which had a distinctive "Ah-oo-ga" cell tone. Omar picked it up and moved into the next room, talking in low tones.

"Your father was promoted to a new gang task force," Bernestine said proudly. "But you never know when you're going to be called," she said ruefully.

"Excuse me," Omar said loudly. "Hold on." His voice started rising until everyone at the table just looked at each other. "That's BS, there's no such thing!" he yelled at the top of his voice. "He must be a junkie and on some kind of drugs. That's crazy talk," Omar scoffed.

Miles was puzzled as he eavesdropped. This sounded odd.

"Ok, I'll be right over," Omar said. "Give me thirty minutes," he finished, jabbing at a button and returning to the table.

"What the hell is the world coming to? Now we have flying saucers shooting at people. A gang member brought into the hospital claimed he was shot by a flying saucer. I'm gonna have to go to the hospital and talk to that fool. Damn drugs are killing us off one at a time!" he snorted. He stood up, cramming in a big bite for the road.

Miles couldn't help himself. "Someday the skies are going to be filled with drones, and that day is coming all too quick," baiting his father.

This infuriated Omar, who immediately glared back. "You don't know what you're talking about, and nobody asked you."

"I know more than you think I do, and if you take the time to listen, you could learn something, too" Miles countered boldly.

Bernestine sensed trouble. She attempted to run interference, saying something hopeful. "If I can get my groceries delivered to my front door, that would be nice," she said.

But it failed. Omar shouted over her as he often did. "Nothing good coming from them things," he yelled. "Sooner or later the gangs will be using drones to drop drugs into prisons and move cash around the city. They'll have more eyes on us that we got on them! I'd like to ban 'em from the skies!"

"Dad, if you can't beat 'em, why not join 'em," Miles said calmly.

"You just get a job, boy!" he yelled. Then Omar got up, grabbed his keys and coat, and muttered his way out the door.

Miles disgruntled, made his way to the kitchen and started doing some dishes, as it was one of his chores.

Kenny asked if he could go down the block and play with one of his friends.

"Be back before dark," was the reply.

Kenny jumped up and left leaving Bernestine to stare out the window into the night sky. She was still lost in thought after Miles had finished loading the dishwasher, fired it up, and stomped upstairs to his room.

CHAPTER 11: Rogue Drones

Walking upstairs, Bernestine took a deep breath and knocked on Miles, door. When he didn't respond, she slowly opened the door, expecting the worst. She looked left then right, but he was not in his room. Walking over to the window, she noticed that boards were missing from the railing and she could faintly see Miles in the sunset. She made her way over quietly, but a squeaky sound startled Miles, who quickly turned around in shock.

"How did you get over here?" he asked, looking back across the bridge.

"The same way you did. When did you make that thing, anyway?"

Miles looked back over his shoulder staring off into the sunset. He ignored her question and asked one of his own. "Why does Dad hate me so much? I haven't done anything wrong."

"He doesn't hate you son, it's just that he's under so much pressure. There is just so much gang activity. Being overworked he's uptight now. He just needs some space to work out this problem, or he could lose his new job before he even gets started."

"He sounds like he's taking it out on me," Miles complained. "If he'd just listen, I could tell him a thing or two," Miles said, head down and fidgeting.

"What do you mean?" she asked sharply, while walking around in front of Miles. "And what is that thing you are working on?" she continued, moving closer.

"It's ok mom, it's just a harmless little toy. I call her *"The Finisher."*

"You know your father is against that," she said nervously.

"Mom, everyone has one now, and I tell you it's not pretty what they can do. I wish Dad wasn't so old," he said wistfully. "This is happening."

She chose calming words to settle him. "He's not that old, Miles. He hurts whenever there's another shooting or stabbing. He was pretty shook up when Kenny got hurt. It eats at him that he hasn't made an arrest in an attack on his own son. Or when there's an unsolved shooting so close to our house."

Miles slumped his shoulders. "Yeah, I know," he said. He wanted to say more, but he instead launched his drone, which momentarily frightened his mother.

"Oh!" she cried out."

"Don't worry, it's fine. You want to see what it looks like? Come over here and stand next to me. Don't worry, it's not going to hurt you, and you're not gonna fall off the roof. We don't move, just the drone."

Reluctantly, she stood next to Miles and observed the screen he was pointing at. To her amazement, she could see everything it was doing. "There's a camera mounted on it. Now look closely, I'll stop it and turn it around and do a 360, then point it back at us," he said with a smile. "Go ahead and wave. You'll see yourself."

Bernestine waved and was speechless as she watched Miles and herself on the screen.

"Watch this. You see that building with the lights on about a mile away in that direction?"

"Yes, why?"

"Put these goggles on and it'll help you see more clearly." With that Miles directed the drone toward the building. Within a few minutes, the drone was circling the building and Miles stopped it at some distance from the windows. He zoomed in and soon they were watching the night janitor dancing with his vacuum while vacuuming a carpet. He had on a headset and swirled the vacuum around like a ballroom dancer.

Bernestine just stared at Miles, not knowing what to say until he broke the silence. "This is what the future holds mom. Here, look at this button. Press it for me."

"No! Absolutely not," she said, stepping backward. "We got to get better window shades," she muttered.

"It's ok, it won't hurt you," he encouraged, extending his arm with the transmitter.

Hesitantly, she pushed the button and quickly put her arm down.

"Now watch what happens." Within a few minutes, the drone reappeared and hovered within a few feet, and then landed. "See, you did it!" he said excitedly.

She just looked out in the distance, then back at Miles and his drone, thinking. "OK, back we go," she said firmly, as they crossed back over the bridge.

"Don't tell Dad yet, ok? I'll figure out something," Miles promised. She nodded and said goodnight, and left him alone with his thoughts.

The next morning Omar was sitting at the table drinking coffee and reading the local newspaper. Miles came down and gave his Dad a pat on the shoulder. "How'd it go?" he asked. He hoped to avoid a new argument, so he tried a new tack.

Omar was already worked up, but he wasn't mad at Miles for a change. "There was another gang battle last night, with multiple deaths and casualties. The gang task force has been activated statewide, and I'm being assigned to a command center with ability to centralize our resources. We're fighting back," he said proudly.

"With what, a donut gun?" Miles joked, instantly regretting it.'

Omar erupted. "We got manpower, we got computers, we got money this time. We'll get 'em," he yelled.

"Dad, you got nothin'. While you talk on radios, they use cell phones. While you drive Fords, they drive Maserati's. While you log on from a tower, they stay mobile with laptops. You're using carrier pigeons and they got drones."

Omar was getting madder. "You don't know anything about us. We got our toys."

Bernestine settled Omar down with a look. "Honey, I saw something last night that not only scared me but may have some relevance to what's been happening."

Miles bugged out his eyes. He realized that she never agreed to his request to keep their secret. He inwardly groaned.

Omar turned his full attention to her. "What are you talking about?" he asked, concerned.

"Miles stopped flying those airplanes at the park, just like you told him. But he didn't stop flying. He's got a new drone that he uses to keep an eye on the whole neighborhood, he calls it *The Finisher*. He's pretty good with it, too. Instead of ignoring him and pushing him away, you maybe ought to see what he's been up to."

Bernestine walked out of the room, leaving Omar glaring at Miles. "That all true?" he asked

"Mom don't lie, you know that," Miles said calmly.

Omar stared out the window. He was going to be late for work, but he didn't budge. "All over the neighborhood? *The Finisher*?"

Miles nodded.

"All right, let's take a look," Omar said, and they went upstairs.

Looking around the room Omar noticed all the trophies, ribbons and pictures of Miles with his drones and friends. "Looks like you're pretty good at this stuff, aren't you?" he said while picking up a strange looking drone. A little pride may have slipped into his tone, Miles thought.

"That's *Sparrow*," Miles said. "She's one of the earlier versions of a racing drone. She'll fly about forty-miles to fifty miles per hour, and she can do a few simple tasks."

Omar said nothing, but he was dialed in and listening.

Miles continued. "This is a Felix-8 I won in a tournament," he said, pointing to the bigger bird. "She's my pride and joy; I call her *The Finisher*. She'll go 45 miles an hour, and you have to wear special goggles to see where she's going or to view it on this transmitter screen."

"It's got a camera?" Omar asked.

"Yeah, for scouting and just flying around the sky. It can do a few tricks, and even pack things around. I can send her about three miles from where you're standing, and it'll automatically come back to you once you push the button on the transmitter. It has a special camera on it for recording videos or pictures, and later you can pull out the SD card and play it back on the computer."

At this point, Miles happened to look down and saw one of the barrels for his AR-15 sticking out from under his bed. Quickly he distracted his dad and slid the gun further back. He tried to stop himself from shaking.

Omar looking around the room and with a smile looked back at his son. With a deep sigh, he relaxed. "I'm sorry for being an ass lately but this case has just about ruined my life. It's changing me, and I hate it, but there is just so much to do. I feel like the dams going to burst and all I have is a finger to hold it back."

"Yeah, I get it," Miles said. "Keep fighting, Dad," he said softly.

Omar brightened. "So, does this make sense? We're seeing robberies now of hobby stores. They're not taking cash, they're grabbing gear. Drone gear."

"Somebody must be tired of paying retail," Miles smiled. "This stuff adds up. I've been lucky to win my gear, but every time I crash, I have to worry about spare parts."

"Yeah," Omar said, thinking.

"C'mon, let me show you a few things," Miles said. They went out to the roof, and Miles handed his Dad the spare goggles. "Put these on," he commanded. "You'll need them while I look at this monitor on the transmitter."

Miles launched *The Finisher* into the air and put her through a few tricks. He sent her out almost as far as it would go, taking it around barriers, tall trees, and buildings. He held her at some different altitudes while spinning the craft around for the full 360-degree view, and Omar chuckled. He even dove the drone towards the ground at full speed, then immediately pulled out, saying, "Oops."

Then he bought the drone home with his hands on his side. "No hands," he bragged. As it approached, he told his dad, "Watch this. She'll land all by herself."

Omar handed the goggles to his son and whistled. "We need one of those," he said with conviction. They made their way back to the computer, and Miles popped out the SD card, inserted it into his laptop, and brought up the new file.

Omar checked his watch, shrugged, and watched the screen. Before the video loaded, he saw that Miles had been working on his application to the High School to Flight School Program. He nodded approvingly, but said nothing.

For the next few minutes, they watched just what they had done with the drone. Omar reacted to the spins and flips like a kid, and Miles was happy. "It may be a fad, but unfortunately not everyone is doing legal stuff with these drones.

"What do you know about the illegal stuff? What are you talking about?"

Miles reached into his drawer and pulled out the incriminating SD card, stared at his dad, then pushed it in. The video started off with a drone race, but quickly switched and went blank. Then a new image appeared, but it was out of focus and dark. Gradually it sharpened, and Omar could see it was from a drone starting a sortie, climbing off the roof then pointing down the street.

Omar leaned forward as the video showed the entire crime right down the street from where they lived. Miles then stopped the video and looked at his dad, who just sat horror-struck.

"You know what you've done?" Omar finally blurted out. "You're a witness to a murder! What the hell were you thinking? We have to turn that in, because holding evidence like this will get you put in jail, and I'll get fired!" Omar seethed.

"There's more Dad. You should probably know it all."

"What do you mean more?"

"You have to promise you'll let me explain everything before you arrest me," Miles pleaded.

Fearing the worst, Omar just sat back in his chair. "What did you do?" he demanded.

"I went and fetched the murder weapon," Miles admitted.

"Shit, shit, shit! What the hell? You knew about all of this stuff and you didn't say a word? What happened to the gun? Where is it?"

Slowly Miles reached down under the bed and pulled out the AR-15 pistol with all its components. "That's what I have been trying to tell you all along. If I can figure out how to do it, you know the gang-bangers have already thought about it. Gangs are already using drones to shoot each other, but they haven't discovered the techniques for shooting multiple rounds like I have," he added for conclusion.

Omar grew calm. "We need to box up everything and head down to the police station right now," he said, in a tone that didn't include any doubt. "Now!"

On the way in, Omar's cell phone rang out. He put it on speaker so he could drive. "Omar, it's bad. There was a fake truce late last night, and the two parties showed up for a meeting and all hell broke loose. It was an ambush by drones. We got a few statements, and there was a crashed drone on the ground that we found. You need to get down here!"

When Omar and Miles arrived at the police station with the box in tow, the commander was already worked up. He was an older, heavy-set Black man, with white hair at the temples and not even a trace of a smile. While Miles waited at his Dad's desk, Omar and Commander Lewis were shouting in a conference room. Miles could not help but hear the commotion.

"What the hell is happening out there?" Commander Lewis yelled. "This keeps getting worse!"

Omar raised his voice, too. "Give us some help," he pleaded. "The technology out there is killing us. We're sending up carrier pigeons and they've got drones!"

Miles smiled. It was his exact line! Maybe his Dad really was listening!

"You need to get on top of this right now, you hear?" the commander yelled at the top of his voice. " I want answers. Don't come back until you have something to offer! You're dismissed, dammit."

Omar didn't budge. "Commander, I believe I already have something so incredible, you won't believe your eyes," Omar said. He got up and moved to leave the room. "I want you to see this, sir," he said, motioning toward his desk.

"What is it?" the commander asked, following him.

"Well, it's a bit awkward. My son has been doing a little police work on his own, it appears. I'm asking for full immunity for him, because, uh, let's just say he didn't exactly follow procedures. But he's got something," Omar added.

The commander was old-school, and he didn't believe in sugar-coating anything. "You better hope to hell that this has some relevance to this case, or I'll have your ass and your badge, son," the agitated commander growled. They both stood over Miles, who wanted to disappear.

"Show him the video, son," Omar said calmly. He couldn't imagine what Miles must be feeling. "I know you're scared, and this day isn't going the way you thought it would. I'll write you a note for school. Just show the Chief that little movie."

Miles fumbled for the SD card in its protective sleeve and looked around for his Dad's computer. It was a tower, sitting on the floor, and it had a floppy drive on the front.

"A floppy drive? Seriously? So, no SD reader?" he muttered. Fortunately, he had his laptop in his backpack, and he quickly set it up and brought it to life. He slid the card in decided that he didn't want to move the file to his Dad's PC, so he loaded the movie straight from the card.

They all leaned in as the video played yet again.

The commander was speechless for once. Omar chimed in. "I imagine the district attorney will tell us there is no way we could use that video," he said reluctantly.

The chief agreed. "No, you'd need a warrant." He turned to Miles. "How did you get this?" he asked. He seemed strangely calmer, Miles thought.

For the next hour and a half, told most of what he knew. He pulled out various props from the cardboard box and explained the technology in the simplest terms. He explained how he made his drones run dark and quiet, and how he worked out the mechanical engineering for the remote firing device. He showed them the bump stock, the suppressor, and the various clips, and explained how he stole them. It felt like a weight was being lifted from his shoulders as he went through his testing and simulation trials.

When he was done, Commander Lewis turned to Omar. "I ought to arrest his little ass on the spot! Do you know how serious this is? I'm taking possession of all this stuff. What a mess! Omar, get him out of here! I'll decide whether or not I'm gonna charge him with obstruction, you understand?" he shouted, shaking his head and again looking at the table of evidence.

Omar objected. "I thought about this, sir. If we chalk it up to a citizen just trying to help, we can keep a lid on it. But I think there's a better angle."

Miles just stared. So, did the commander.

Omar kept going. "We've never seen anything like this before, right? Gunfights with drones? What ever happened to the good ole days when we took ten paces turned and fired? At least people looked each other in the eye while firing. Now they look at a screen and tell a drone to do the shooting from God knows where. This is some scary shit, and to be able to buy this crap off the web, legally too? Damn, we're in way over our heads. Well, let's fight back. Let's use this break."

The chief was confused. "Go on," he finally said.

"Look, this explains all those hobby store robberies. The gangs are going for the most expensive drones and spare parts. Maybe we can set a trap, or jam their frequencies, or spy on the spies. I don't know; I'm still thinking. But we're fighting a forest fire with a squirt gun. Let's get in the game."

Commander Lewis wasn't convinced, but he as at least leaning. "OK, maybe. Write it all up and have a proposal on my desk in twenty-four hours. And get that kid back in school!"

They rode mostly in silence, both lost in thought. Miles finally broke the silence. "I'm sorry if I got you in trouble, I..." but he was immediately interrupted.

"What you did was wrong, there's no doubt about it. But maybe some good can come of it." Arriving at school, Omar parked and looked at Miles. "This is gonna get real ugly, and I mean quick. Don't you tell anyone about this and I mean anyone. I don't want your life endangered, you hear me?" he commanded.

"Yes, sir I understand." The rest of the day was a blur.

CHAPTER 12: Misfortune

Miles entered the next drone race with a weird feeling. This race was being touted as the race of the season, but summer was gone, and it was a dreary, dismal day. The smell of fried food didn't move him, and the music didn't perk him up, either. He barely acknowledged Ralph and Katie. Instead of a day full of trial heats and elimination rounds, this was one, single race. It was just as well, he thought. He needed to get home.

Katie, Ralph, and Miles were going head to head, which should have fired up his competitive juices, but it didn't. He went through the motions, prepping for battle, but he kept thinking about his dad's boss. The old bull scared him, he admitted.

He had a new drone he'd put together from spare parts that he used only for racing; she was named *Falcon*, short for the *Millennium Falcon*. Once he got her on the starting line, he felt himself focus better. He started humming the first few bars of *Pushing Mach 5*, and settled in. Five, four, three, two, one and they were off amongst a group of ten. Each lap was filled with drones bouncing off the wall of the abandoned factory, some falling out of the sky as if shot, and others going out of control off the course and being disqualified. Miles played it cool, skipping any chance to accelerate or take risks, and avoiding crash after crash. He put on a burst of speed at the end to finish strong, just like always, and was surprised to find himself up near the leaders.

When the last lap was completed, it was so close that the judges had to review the photo finish to determine the winner. To his surprise, it was Katie who inched past Ralph and Miles to win.

The racers all retired to a big table and dug in hungrily to a feast of sandwiches, chips, cookies, and sodas. Miles recognized Jeff, who was describing one of his most epic crashes. Jeff was a younger white teenager with wild hair and a bit of a surfer vibe, who apparently liked to push hard. Ralph told Jeff he needed to play it cool at the start, and never take risks at the wrong time.

"Life is a risk, Ralph," Jeff responded. "You never know, so you have to go for the gusto!" he added with a grin.

As the trophies were handed out, Miles got a good-natured punch on the shoulder from Katie. "You're getting better, dude," she said sweetly. Miles blushed, then grew annoyed at his embarrassment. Then he got mad at himself for getting mad. She just laughed.

As the party was dying down, three individuals were taking a keen interest in Miles and Katie. They were pretty rough-looking homies, with tattoos and chains and other unmistakable gang signs. One was bald, one had short dreads, and the other had a short clip with a large, bleached spot on the side of his head and a front row of shiny gold teeth. From afar, Ralph eyed them warily as they approached his friends, but he kept his distance.

Miles was distracted by one of the sponsors and walked away. When he glanced back, it looked as though Katie was involved in an animated conversation with the three men. They spoke in hushed tones, but she grew angrier, and ended up yelling "Take off, you losers! Get out of my face!"

Miles relaxed, at first fearing they were hitting on her. They walked away and she joined Miles and Ralph.

"What up, Katanator?" Ralph asked.

She shrugged. "I just got a job offer," she said evenly.

Miles and Ralph both stared at her, then back at the homies, who were stepping up into large, black SUV, which quickly roared away.

"You came in third," Ralph pointed out.

"And they say chivalry is dead," she glared. "Maybe they have an EEO plan?"

"Not that you're not a good flyer," Ralph said, trying to recover.

"It's ok," she said. "I think they were just trying to cut me from the herd. Metal Mouth asked me if I'd fly for him. They call themselves the Bunker Buster Boys. Said he'd give me the latest drones and all the extra equipment I ever wanted. Even said I'd get all the fringe benefits. Yeah, I know what benny's he's talking about," she smirked. "I don't think they have health care or a pension plan, tho."

"What'd you say?" Miles asked. "Those dudes are trouble."

"I told him to get lost, but I doubt if he got the message. I'm sure they'll be back." She looked around. "Anyway, this party sucks. I'm outa here. Don't grip your joysticks too hard," she added, sauntering off with her trophy sticking out of her small backpack.

Miles and Ralph talked on the way home, rehashing the race and the discussion with Katie. "What do they need drone pilots for?" Ralph asked. "Think they want to start a league?"

Miles laughed. "Don't be naïve. They're trying to take over the sky. They're moving product, doing recon, snooping on the competition, and more. They've got guns in the air, too, but they haven't figured out how to go full auto yet, from what I can tell."

"Damn," Ralph said. At their final corner, where Miles and Ralph usually went separate ways, Ralph slammed on his brakes. "Hey bro, just wanted to tell ya something. Back at the race when you saw me talking to Katie, well I asked her out and she kind of said 'yeah'."

"Kind of, what does that mean?" Miles replied, somewhat surprised and probably more jealous than he wanted to sound.

"She said to give her a call tomorrow and if she wasn't busy, she'll hang out with me," Ralph said while turning his head away from Miles.

Miles whistled. "Go for it," he blurted out, knowing Ralph was seeking his stamp of approval. "Sorry I didn't think of it myself, you dawg," he added.

They split up, and as he neared home, Miles stopped with a foot on the curb. Off in the distance, above the usual city noise, he heard what he thought were some top-dollar drones making a high-pitched buzzing noise. He couldn't spot them, but he knew there was more than one. He parked his bike and scanned the sky again, but he didn't spot them. He blitzed through the house and went up to his room, but he still couldn't spot the craft. The noise faded.

Ralph was in deep thought, coasting along and still thinking about getting a date with Katie. He, too, heard the sound of advanced drones in the sky. The sound got closer, but when he looked up the trees were blocking his view. It wasn't a Felix-8, he was sure of that. It sounded expensive, with a deeper, richer tone. But who had one of those? And why were they whizzing around the city skies?

He had reached the final intersection before his driveway, but he had to cut the corner on a right turn. He jumped the curb, crossed the sidewalk, and ended up near the center line as he came up to his house on the left. There was that buzz again, closer than ever. He scanned the sky again, but his bike drifted into the path of a rushing delivery truck. The driver hit his brakes, honked his horn, and tried mightily to swerve out of the way, but nothing worked. Ralph slammed into the front of the truck and flew in the air. He landed hard, splitting his bike helmet and literally seeing stars. Blood seeped from his mouth, and he couldn't move. He passed out as the young, blonde truck driver reached him, cell phone already dialing 9-1-1.

The ambulance arrived quickly and they loaded Ralph up carefully, immobilized, before zooming off, sirens blasting. The young truck driver was sobbing as he gave his statement to a young policewoman.

Miles heard the siren from his house, but thought nothing of it. He was very excited when he found his mother, and he immediately sat his backpack down on the couch and pulled out his 3rd place trophy. "Hey mom, third place! I couldn't even beat that stupid girl," he grumbled. "What a great day," he added.

Bernestine reached out and hugged him. "I'm proud of you, son, but I know she isn't stupid" she said softly.

Miles slowed down a bit, still hugging his trophy. "You know what? I'm going to go clean my room and make a nice spot for this!" he announced.

Bernestine could only watch in amusement as he rushed back up the stairs.

At dinner, the phone on their land line rang and Bernestine answered. Her face grew dark almost instantly. "Oh my God, please make him ok," she blurted out.

Miles looked up, and so did Kenny. Omar wasn't home yet, and that was always a concern. She looked terribly upset, and almost in tears. Miles prepared himself for the bad news he thought was about to come. Because of his dad's work, they were right to worry. Once they'd been watching TV without him and the news caster would announce that a policeman had just been killed. They were close to tears of joy when they learned Omar was fine. Was this the time? His stomach churned.

"Is it Dad?" he asked as she hung up the phone?

She shook her head. "No, it's not your dad. It's Ralph" she whispered.

Miles went numb. "What? Is he OK?"

"He got hit by a truck and was taken to the hospital. He's unconscious and in surgery. I'm sure they're doing everything they can," she added, dropping her head.

"It's my fault, it's my fault" he assumed with a deep pain. "If I had made him listen to me earlier about the gangs he'd be ok."

Realizing Miles thought it was Omar she was talking about, she stopped him. "No honey, it's not your daddy, he's ok. It's Ralph. He's been hit by a truck on the way home from the race today. Nobody ever said anything about gangs; it appears to be just a tragic, random accident. His mom said he rode right into the wrong lane."

"What hospital? I have go!" he shouted.

"Don't know. I didn't ask son. Ralph's mom will let us know as soon as they know something. I'm sure he'll be ok," she said, holding Miles close to her.

Miles broke free and ran upstairs, grabbed a heavy coat, and made his way out to the roof where he sat in his chair. The night was cool and foggy, and the air was still. He eventually fell asleep to the sounds of the 'hood.

Later, Omar came home and slumped in a chair. He'd heard about Ralph, and when Miles came down Omar was there for him. They said nothing for a while, just hugging.

Eventually they sat down; Miles took the couch, and Omar sat in his recliner, settling with a small groan. "So, you finish your homework?" Miles heard himself ask. They both chuckled.

"I did. The chief liked my proposal. He boosted me up to second in command to the FBI guy."

"Sounds like you were recruited," Miles smiled. Omar just sat back with his eyes closed. "New job, new boss. Same as the old boss," he sighed.

That reminded Miles of something. "So, dad, something strange happened today at the race. Some 'bangers have been trying to recruit us drone pilots to work for them. That girl Katie I told you about, she got a proposition. They want her to fly for them."

Omar eased himself up. "Do tell," he muttered.

"Yeah, they told her they got all the best stuff, but they need talent. She made it sound like they offered everything but medical and dental."

"Who was it? Any idea?"

"It's our friends" he said sarcastically. "The BBB's. Same ones that shanked Kenny. The funny thing is, they don't know anything about drones or how to fly RC's."

"RC?" Omar questioned.

"It means Remote Control, dad."

"Right. I knew that. How long has this been going on?"

"About a month or so ago they started scoping out the races. We didn't think anything about it until today. Me and Ralph and Katie have been recent winners, so maybe that's why they're interested."

Omar just sat quietly, contemplating what Miles had just told him. "I wonder, just wonder about something," he said, without explaining.

The next morning after church Bernestine took Miles to the hospital while Omar went into the office. Ralph was out of surgery but still very groggy. When he saw Miles, he stirred a bit and was able to talk in short bursts. "Dude!" he coughed.

"You look like hell, homes," Miles joked.

"I know. My bad," Ralph gasped. "Heard a new drone and looked up. Bam!"

Miles digested that, but he felt like he needed to push his friend to think healthy thoughts. "So, can I ask Katie out while you heal up?" Miles said with a grin. "I figure you'll be motivated faster if you think about me and her," he added.

"Rain check," he gasped. "Remember, I seen her first," Ralph added with a grimace. At that point, Ralph's mom told him to rest and motioned to Bernestine to talk outside.

In the hallway Ralph's mother began to cry. "He's alive, but he'll never walk again. The doctor told me he's paralyzed from the waist down. Oh God, what are we going to do?" she wailed.

Bernestine held her tight while they both cried. Going back in the room Miles just stared at Ralph, who had fallen asleep. Bernestine motioned to Miles to leave, and they both gently smiled at Ralph and left, heavy-hearted.

On the way home, Bernestine told Miles that Ralph was paralyzed and would need support if he was going to heal at all. Miles just turned his head, looked out the window at the sky as tears ran down his cheeks. Just before they pulled up at their house, Miles broke his silence. "Dad has got to bust those BBBs. I know it was them that were flying and distracted Ralph."

Shocked, Bernestine said nothing. What was going on in her boy's head? she asked herself.

For the next couple of weeks, Miles thought about Ralph but couldn't bear to visit him. Every time Bernestine suggested it, he'd say something to change the subject. On the fourth day, Miles decided it was time to visit Ralph so he asked his mom to take him. When they arrived at Ralph's room, his bed was empty. They were told he was at physical therapy around the corner. Bernestine told Miles to go on without her, as she would wait there in the room.

Miles thought to himself as he began to walk towards the room and hoped that Ralph would be there walking back and forth. As he peeked around the corner, he was depressed to see him standing between some parallel bars, struggling to remain upright with the help of the therapist. He looked like he was much thinner.

Ralph saw Miles in the mirror before he actually saw him physically. He smiled at Miles, who walked over and just stood there in silence.

"You coming over here or not? I'm not gonna bite you," Ralph said, while reaching out to give Miles five.

Miles gently slapped the outstretched hand.

"Weak, bro. I won't break," Ralph said. They slapped harder.

Miles laughed. "Hey, bro I'm glad to see you," he said slowly.

"Yeah, but not as sorry as I am. I should have been paying more attention to riding instead of looking up at the drones in traffic. It really is true; most accidents happen close to home."

A gifted 17-year old remote-control pilot is drawn into the world of drone racing, only to find himself and friends in an all-out drone war.

Miles laughed. "Drones are going to kill us both," he said.

"I'm not dead. I'll just be stuck in this chair for life," Ralph said, saddened and becoming discouraged.

"You'll walk someday," Miles consoled trying to cheer him up. "We'll put you in a body suit, from *Marvel Comics*. I'll help design it."

"OK, that would rock, wouldn't it?" Ralph felt better already.

"Besides, you can still fly a drone. You ready to go back to your room? I want to see what this baby can do," Miles said, hands on the wheelchair.

"Naw, that's ok, I have to earn to do things for myself, and get stronger. Maybe after wheeling around for a few weeks, my arms are going to be pure muscle," he added, flexing an arm to show off his bicep. They both smiled.

The next couple of weeks were hard on both Miles and Ralph. Both seemed to lose interest in racing, and even Katie said the same thing when Miles ran into her while she was riding her mountain bike.

"Hey Miles, ya want to ride the trails above the rock quarry?"

"Naw, I can't today. Maybe some other time, ok? I gotta see Ralph."

"Sure, whatevs. I heard about him; that's just wrong, wrong, wrong," she said, shaking her head. She looked at him. "Think I should see him?"

"I know he'd like that, but he might not be ready."

"Yeah, good point. I don't want to rush him."

Miles found himself inspecting his shoes and snapped out of it. "Any races coming up?"

Katie shrugged. "You know, without you guys there, it's just not the same. Everyone talks a lot of trash, but they suck as pilots. It's not even a challenge stomping them."

"You are one sassy sister," Miles said with a sly smile.

She laughed and pointed to her T-shirt, which she made easier by sweeping away the two halves of her unzipped sweatshirt. The lettering read "2Hot4U". Miles realized she had made him look at her chest, and he tried not to linger.

"Ain't it the truth," he finally allowed. She gave him a wry grin, probably fully aware of what she'd done.

She got a foot on one pedal and lingered. "Listen, Miles here's my cell phone number if you ever want to fly." She handed him an actual business card, with a drone for a logo and her name and number, plus an email address.

"What the hey?" he said, flipping the card over. It was a light lavender, with bold black lettering and the logo was gold. "I never got a business card from a girl before."

She laughed. "Did you get one from a guy?"

"No," he admitted.

"Just buzz me or give me a chat, ok? Shame about Ralph. When you see him again, tell him 'hi' and to hang in there for me."

Just like that, she was gone.

He looked at the card again, and gave it a sniff. There was a vague perfume smell, or at least some kind of girlieness.

He couldn't help but wonder - by giving him her telephone number, did that mean she wanted him to ask her out for a date? A big smile came over his face as he performed a wheelie and headed off on his bike.

CHAPTER 13: A Father's Request

The newly created task force began meeting regularly on early Sunday morning, but they were unable to obtain any new intel that they could use. There were plenty of rumors that ended up being without any substance, and Omar was getting anxious.

His commanding officer called him into the office after a meeting. "Omar, didn't you tell me that your son said that he thought gang members were actively recruiting drone pilots?"

"Yeah, that's true." Omar's trailed off warily.

"Well, I've been thinking about something I want to share with you. What if your son were to..." but he was interrupted.

"Oh, hell no," Omar chimed in. "I know where you're going with this, and hell, no!"

"Let me finish," his boss demanded. "What if Miles, and say a few of his friends let themselves be recruited, but they worked for us? We'd be able to crack this thing wide open. They'd be protected, I promise you," the commander insisted. "I've already talked to the head of the task force. He's willing, and figures it's safer to have one of our own pilots to infiltrate rather than a brand-new person showing up. Again, I'm pleading for your help on this, Omar."

Omar shook his head. "Boss, at least he doesn't have my last name. If word leaks out about our task force and who's on it, don't you think that could be trouble?"

Commander Lewis hesitated. "Good point. We'll have to finesse that. But I don't think you're too well known yet. If we act fast, we can work it."

Omar was dubious. "I'll think about it, and get back to you."

"Don't take long because plan B is worse."

"What is plan B?" Omar asked.

"You don't want to know."

The task force meeting lasted so long, Omar almost missed church. When he found a seat at the back of Mt. Olivet, several rows behind Bernestine, he was surprised at the amount of youth in the congregation today. He hadn't realized that this was the Sunday that Reverend Jackson was giving a message to the church on youth. The Rev, as he called himself, was in his late forties, but was slim and fit, with a trimmed beard and nice suit. But his eyes dominated his personage; he had an intent, piercing gaze, as though service to the Lord gave him great joy.

Omar looked around. There were very few empty seats. The Rev had done a good job on marketing, he figured.

Once the singing and announcements were out of the way, the Rev got himself worked up quickly. "Our youth are our future," he thundered. "They are our tomorrows. But look at their lives. They are constantly forced to overcome the temptations of the streets." He got an "Amen" for that.

"It is hard to resist the siren call of easy money, pushing drugs and making bank," he thundered. "It is hard to overcome the constant nuisance of insolence and foul language and disrespect. But we have to keep our eyes open and touch our troubled youth," he continued. The crowd murmured, expecting more.

He paused and gathered their attention. "You know kids, you may roll your eyes and think we're out of touch, but remember that we were young once, too. Some of us may look old, we may listen to the wrong tunes, and we may seem to care more about mortgages and our waistlines than we do about what's happening around us. But we haven't forgotten how hard it is to be young. We know about your peer pressure, about the messages you get in your songs, on TV, at the movies. We get it. It was tough for us, too." The crowd agreed with him, and he kept going.

"Just look around ya'll, I am so proud to be your pastor and I am so grateful to the youth who've decided to attend church today to hear the wisdom of God. And to you, the older members who complain about the youth of today, shaking your heads in disgust, I ask you for patience. I ask you for respect. I ask you to help, don't hate. Love, don't laugh. Some of you object to the hoodies you see, or the baggy pants that some youth wear, hanging so low they're a tripping hazard. Some of you shake your heads and roll your eyes," he mocked, pantomiming with exaggerated expressions, which brought out laughter from the congregation.

He paused, and his smile turned serious. "Some of you shake your heads because you expect more reverence to this temple and more respect for this sanctuary. But let me tell you something. Clothing did not walk through these doors; our brethren and sisters made that pilgrimage. And some may have had no choice, being led by the ear or the nose," he smiled, and the crowd chuckled.

"I remember the day when ties and suits and dresses were the dress code here. I even remember whispers about who had what money, judging by the flashy jewelry, the flamboyant hats and the expensive cars parked in the front so everyone could see how lavish we appear. Now, I'm being honest today, I'm just saying. Remember ya'll, its needs versus traditions. We don't feel the pain of our youth, because we're too busy causing the pain," he scolded. With a deep breath Rev Jackson just sighed. "Can I get an amen, ya'll?"

The church all chimed in "Amen."

Omar had drifted off in his own thoughts, and was brought back by the congregation joining in with a thunderous amen as he peered at the backs of the youth from his perch. He thought about the reminder of how impressionable kids are, and how they have become the "techie" generation. Kids now days have to have the biggest, newest toys. How easy it is to get hooked on video games, computers, cell phones, all that. No wonder there seemed to be a growing distance between kids and their parents.

Ruefully, he realized he was one of those parents he thought and how did this happen? Long hours, missed meals, missing out on the kids growing up...ouch. This task force has taken away all my time, he realized. As the choir broke out with the departing song, he stood up, joined in and his eyes met Bernestine, Miles and Kenny. With a broad smile, he nodded in their direction as he waited for them to meet him at the back of the church. "Hey hun, how about you and Kenny drive home together. I'm gonna take Miles with me." Bernestine was surprised, but agreed, while Miles looked perplexed. Kenny felt he got the short end of the ride and wanted to go with his dad and Miles, but that was quickly put down.

"I'll take Kenny out for some donuts and meet you back at the house," she said while smiling at Kenny.

As they drove in silence, Omar was thinking about how to talk to Miles without them getting into their usual verbal squabbles. He turned into the park, driving past the soccer field and pulled into a stall. "You want to go for a walk?" he suggested.

Miles defensively agreed, with a classic passive-aggressive "Whatever," and opened the door to get out. To their amazement a few kids were flying drones. Immediately, Miles began critiquing them as they went through their paces. "They're ok pilots, but you can tell they haven't been flying long. Listen to them, no steady speed, slow, then fast. That's a sign of a new pilot not having the confidence to take those tight corners at a constant speed. They're just doing wide loops or going downwind and turning around and trying to come back. Just like that one over there by the net, watch. Just what I thought, rammed it right into the goalie net. That happens a lot when you're learning."

"Did that happen to you when you were learning to fly?"

"Oh yeah, and it still does as you learn new things" Miles replied with a smile.

"When did you get into flying drones?"

Miles thought for a minute thinking ok, here it comes but he looked out at the drones. "Remember when Kenny got hurt that day and you told me I couldn't fly helicopters or airplanes anymore? Well, I never flew them again, but that's when I started flying drones," he admitted, in an attempt to cover up or justify his defiance.

Omar surprised Miles when he corrected him. "Actually, I meant no more flying remote-control aircraft. You know, RC's," he added while staring at the shocked look on Miles' face. As they both stood in silence it was time to reveal the plan. This wasn't going to be easy.

"You know I've been working long hours on the new gang task force. We're at a crossroads and can't get a handle on what's really going on. I met with the commander and he's putting a plan together and it'll involve getting some expert drone pilots to work on our team."

"There's a lot of good pilots out there, so it should be easy to find some." Miles kept watching the drones.

"Yeah but gangs are getting smarter now days and they can spot a plant pretty easily, and from what you've said they're out there recruiting as we talk. They have to be up to something pretty big, and that's why this is getting to be rather urgent. So, you interested in getting involved?"

This brings a huge laugh from Miles, who just shook his head.

Defensively Omar blurted out. "I should have guessed that you'd say no."

"I didn't say anything, I just laughed" he professed. But before Omar could reply, Miles looked at him. "So, what do you need?" he asked.

"We need three or four good pilots that we can trust to keep their mouths shut and will take direction. This is going to get ugly and dangerous. You in?"

"Yeah, I'm in and think I can recommend two of my friends as well. There's one girl who can really fly. She's always beating the boys and laughing at us. Her name is Katie Slauson. There's another pilot, Ralph Stenson."

"Ralph? He's the one that is paralyzed, right? I don't think he'll do, he's in a wheel chair."

"So, what?" Miles blurted out defensively. "He's paralyzed from the waist down not his arms and hands," Miles emphasized. "Besides, he needs something like this because he's in a deep funk."

"Well, I dunno son, I dunno."

"Will you please just think about what I've said?" he implored while shaking his head in disbelief. "I've never asked you for anything, at least not as important as this. It'll mean a lot to me," he pleaded.

As they both looked across the field, another drone crashed with such force you could see pieces scattering about. Omar relented. "Ok, I'll see what I can do, but I can't promise Ralph will be accepted."

CHAPTER 14: Do Something

After a series of phone calls and meetings all week, Omar finally got approval to keep moving forward recruiting the kids. Because of the secrecy of this undertaking, it was determined that Miles would contact Katie first.

The good news was that the task force approved the purchase of a pair of new Felix-9 drones, and Miles got to put one through its paces all week. By Sunday after church, he was set.

Omar didn't get home until well after church, but he felt like he had good news. When Miles was informed that he could make the contact with Katie, he was thrilled. His secret crush on Katie wouldn't go away, and he missed being around her. But he wasn't able to gather the courage to call her until now.

"Hey dad, I have her telephone number. She gave it to me a few weeks ago and said to call her if I got bored and we could fly together, so I can do this." Miles grew excited, and he went upstairs to make the call.

"Katie, it's Miles. What up?"

Katie seemed genuinely happy to hear from him. "Nothin much," she admitted. "Whatcha got?"

"Meet me over at the abandoned warehouse and I'll show you," he teased. "Be there in an hour?"

"Sure, I'll be there," she confirmed.

Omar and Commander Kelley dropped off Miles with his bike and a big box at the meeting spot. It was a derelict building that was a bit dark, but it didn't smell of garbage or worse. It was actually fairly tidy, as though it was prepped for sale. Miles emptied the box, turned it upside down to act as a table, and checked his breath to see if he was ok. He caught a whiff of his armpits, and frowned. Oh, well.

As Katie rode her bike into the large vacant area, she recognized Miles off in the distance. He waved her on to where he was standing. "Hey-0 Katie" he said warmly. "Glad you could make it," he said, while trying not to stare at her pink T-shirt. He couldn't quite read it.

"Yeah, my pleasure. What's that on the makeshift table?" she asked, moving in closer.

"Oh, it's a little something I thought we'd like to fly. I've got a new sponsor of sorts, and they want me to test fly it. That's the course over there, painted and taped off."

"Really? What gang you belong to?" She followed up by saying, "Just kidding." Little did she know that he really had signed up to be in a gang; they just dressed better.

Thinking quickly, Miles looked at the table. "Pick out the one you want. I'll show you what gang I belong too. It's called first place," he said with a grin.

"You're on," she said fiercely, bending down and picking out the bright-colored green drone. "All the goggles look alike, so I'll take these," she said, expertly setting herself up.

Peering at Katie, who had removed her light blue hoodie, he now had full view of her T-shirt. It read "Looking for Wing Man" in gold lettering. As she adjusted to look back, he turned his head away embarrassed, because he got caught staring. He broke the spell.

"Notice the paint job on these drones? They've been sprayed with a very light fluorescent paint that makes them glow brightly, even under low light. You'll see when we blow through the shadows."

She seemed impressed, but held back.

Miles tried to get her into it. "Go ahead take a lap to get used to the new transmitter and drone. I've already tried mine."

Katie launched her drone, and after the first lap, complimented Miles on the new equipment. "Handles pretty good. Bet I hit fifty miles an hour."

"Yeah, and you didn't push the throttle down all the way, either. In the manual it says it'll shoot up to around eighty-five. So fast you couldn't fly these without special goggles with a new HD and a wider field of vision."

Katie walked over to the starting point, laid her drone down and walked back.

"Enough talking, let's do it," she said confidently. "I'll count us off because I know you can't count," she mocked. "Five laps should give you the opportunity to chase me around."

"Ok, but the winner gets the drone. Come to think of it, the loser gets one as well," he relayed with a laugh.

"Five, four, three, two, one!" Katie shouted as they both took to the air. It was a battle all the way to the end. He knew he was more familiar with the Felix-9, and that was all the advantage he needed. He took an early lead, but she hung right on his right flank. They twisted and jostled through the course, jockeying for the lead, but Miles was always able to fend her off. Finally, near the end Miles punched it and won by five or six yards.

Katie took off her headset and gulped some air. Her cheeks glowed red, and her eyes sparkled. "Wow! That was awesome, Miles," she said with a mock bow. "Kudus to you! Great race!"

Her comment stunned him, and he didn't know how to respond. But he had to say something, because he needed the courage to ask her to be on their team. So, the recruitment message began. He knew how to ease into it.

"So, Katie, any more of them jerks bothering you about joining their so-called clubs?"

She waved him off. "No, I must have scared them away. If it were up to me, I'd use drones and hunt them down and take them all out. Pump a Hellfire up their tailpipe. I'm sick and tired of them. You can't walk up and down the street without them trying to hit on you. They've taken over the parks and all night long, you hear tires screeching and gun shots and ambulances. I want to move out of this hell-hole so bad, but my mom and dad have good jobs and they said they'd be damned if they were going to be chased out of the neighborhood by thugs."

Miles took the bait and quickly responded. "What if you *could* do something, would you? I mean, if there was a way to stop the violence, or get them under control, would you?"

"Come on. You on weed? There isn't anything we could do to stop this madness."

"No, I'm serous. If we could, would you?"

"For the sake of argument, yeah I would. So now what?"

Out of the shadows came two individuals, which startled Katie, but Miles quickly put her at ease. "This is my dad and his boss," he said as they moved closer. Katie stood her ground, ready for any perceived confrontation and her body language showed it. Was there anything she was afraid of? he wondered.

For the next thirty minutes, Omar informed Katie about the task force, its rationale for existing, and the need to get someone inside the gangs.

Katie kept looking at Miles the entire time and finally asked if Ralph had joined this team. "You in?" she pressed him.

He admitted that he was. "Yep. And you're the first one I thought of."

She thought for a few seconds, then nodded her head. Omar said they needed to hear it in words. Katie smiled and gave a resounding "Yes!"

She was told they'd be in touch and needed her to swear to its secrecy. As she was about to leave, Miles pointed to her new drone. "You earned that, lady," he said.

She was surprised that he had actually meant it. "Seriously?"

Miles nodded. "Don't lose it, because it cost a lot of cash," he said with a genuine smile.

Later on that evening, Omar and Miles talked as equals. Miles finally understood some of what drove his Pops to fight crime, to do good.

"Are you going to talk to Ralph tonight?" Omar asked. "We need to get everyone on board as soon as possible to start this planning."

"I haven't talked to Ralph lately. I tried to ask him if he'd join the club, but I didn't hear back from him. I'll text him again and then go over." Looking down at his cell phone he actually saw a message from Ralph, but it was cryptic and didn't make any sense. "Death From Above," it said.

Miles shrugged. He tapped in "What up, dawg?" then replied. Ralph responded curtly. "Called it a night. Check you later."

Miles could understand if he didn't really feel like having any company, but this couldn't wait. When he shared the message with his dad, Omar frowned.

"It sounds to me like a friend needs a friend," he said softly.

Miles jumped on his bike and headed over to Ralph's. As he rode, he saw a group of thugs roughing each other up in front of a small, ramshackle house. He stayed away and dashed by safely. In the distance, sirens wailed, moving away to his practiced ear. Arriving at Ralph's, he rang the familiar door bell.

Mrs. Stenson answered the door, gave him a hug, and told him she was glad he had come over. She motioned him to the family room and said she'd bring out some snacks. Walking over to the French doors, he paused, knowing it was going to be rough. He took a deep breath and opened the doors.

"Hey bro, what's shakin'? Haven't seen you in a while, and was in the hood and thought I'd pop in," he said breezily, hoping for a good response.

"I sent you a text saying I didn't want any company," Ralph fumed.

"Stupid phone; didn't see it," Miles claimed. He tapped at his phone a few times for emphasis. "I must need a new phone," he added for effect.

He glanced around at the disarray; there were several drones in front of Ralph, but they all looked like they'd been torn apart. He picked up a micro and reminisced. "Wow, I remember this little guy. It's the one you taught me how to fly with."

Still no response from Ralph. "My first race, you came up to me and said don't fly the mini but fly the micro. Thanks to you I won that group," he continued, attempting to get a response.

Finally, Ralph spoke up. "Then you can have it! In fact, you can take them all! I don't want to ever fly again. I'm through," he declared with a detached look.

Miles ignored his declaration. "You remember when you said to me if I ever need you, I could count on you?"

"Yeah, I remember," Ralph said quietly. "But that was then, and this is now. What good am I now like this?" he asked, turning his back on Miles. "I can't even sleep in my own bedroom. I had to be put in the TV room. I can't even get upstairs if I wanted to."

"Yeah, but look at all the space you have in here," Miles pointed out. "I wish I had this much room," he said, trying to cheer up Ralph. There was an awkward pause.

"Anyway, to the point. I need you. I'm about to get involved with the biggest race of my life, and I'm afraid, really afraid what will happen if we lose."

"What do you mean if *we* lose?" Ralph said. He wasn't sniveling anymore, Miles noted.

"It's serious, dude, and if we win, this is going to affect the entire community. It's that big. But it's all at risk of going down the tubes. I need your help."

Ralph made a face. "That makes no sense at all. What are you saying?"

"You got to fly with me, Ralph."

"Man, I can't even walk. Look at me. I'm useless." Miles cursed. Ralph was back to feeling sorry for himself.

Ralph's mother was about to enter with some refreshments. Hearing Ralph whining, and Miles overcoming every objection, made her smile. She paused, then decided to wait behind the door a bit more, listening.

Miles walked around to face Ralph. "Yeah, I can see that, I'm not blind! You still have two good arms and hands, don't you? You aren't dead, dammit, but you're stuck in this room afraid of life!

You promised me if I ever needed you, you'd be there. Well, Ralph, I need you to fly. I really do."

Ralph realized he had never seen Miles this emotional before. That checked his next "Yeah but" in mid breath. He just stared at his friend, and he felt himself just kind of give up. "Ok, ya whiner. What is it? What do you want?"

Composing himself, Miles smiled at Ralph. "I need you to meet me tomorrow at this new vacant warehouse. I need you to fly the course with me. I need your advice and how we can help this neighborhood, that's what I need! It'll only take a couple of hours and afterwards, if you want to come back to stay in this room, I won't stop you. Ok? But I'm telling you, bro you need to get out of here and get some fresh air. Whew, I smell your feet."

"Man, that's your smelly armpits and you know it," Ralph shot back.

Miles checked his right pit and laughed. "You got me," he laughed. "So, you in?"

Ralph shrugged. "Will you get out of my house if I say 'yes'?"

"I will. I have a friend who has a van who will pick you up if you want, and bring you back home."

"I dunno," came a weak response.

"Just promise me you'll think about it, ok?"

Mrs. Stenson timed her entrance just right. She came in with a plate of peanut butter cookies and some milk. It lightened the mood to the point that Ralph asked what time he needed to be ready in the morning if he actually decided to follow through.

Miles said he would text him with the specific information, and also told Ralph that Omar would be calling for a chat to fill him in on the details. Guessing that was his cue to leave, he wiped the milk from his mouth on his sleeve, cookie in tow, and gave Ralph's mother a big hug and a high five. He slapped Ralph's hand next, and then he stopped.

"By the way. Katie is in as well."

Getting no response Miles grabbed another cookie. He turned to look at Ralph. "She told me to tell you she misses ya, but I don't know why?" he added with a grin. Then he was gone.

That evening Ralph rolled himself over to the box of drones, pulled out the micro and began to fly it back and forth in the room, while his mother smiled from the other room, listening to the sounds of happiness.

CHAPTER 15: Operation Sky Hawk

When Miles arrived, the warehouse where he had recently out-raced Katie had taken on a new transformation. You could see people scurrying around at the far end, coming and going from multiple rooms. Miles saw his dad dart down a hallway, but then he was gone again. So he turned to one of the drones that was still in a box and started piecing it together.

In a few minutes, Omar came walking over, advising Miles that there was a lot going on and to stay on this end of the building. "Oh, and keep an eye out for Ralph," he added.

Katie came riding through the door, screeching her tires and leaving a three-foot black skid mark on the floor. "Hey, what's hummin', Miles?"

"Ah, nothing much, just waiting for Ralph to show up."

"You really think he'll show?"

At that moment, the garage door opened and a van with a magnetic construction sign pulled into the parking stall. The rear end opened and a ramp unfolded with mechanical precision. Then Ralph came down, telling the plainclothes officer assisting him to stop fussing. "I can do this myself, thanks," he added testily.

"Just like Ralph, huh?" Miles chimed in.

Katie laughed. "Yep. Still feisty." Ralph rolled over strongly, coming to a stop.

"Nice wheels," Katie said admiringly. "How fast will it go?"

Ralph actually smiled. "I still need to work on that a bit," he admitted.

"You look good, bud," she told him.

Miles was sure he saw Ralph blush.

"Thanks, Katie lady," Ralph said. "What's your shirt say today?"

Katie unzipped her hoodie. "American Made" she read aloud.

"I didn't know you were so patriotic," Ralph mocked.

"Blame him," she said, pointing to Miles. "And look around."

Ralph did so. "What is all this?" he asked.

"Oh, it's just an empty warehouse," Miles said, looking around.

"Yeah, it doesn't look empty to me," Ralph said. Then he saw the drone Miles was assembling. "No way – the Felix 9?"

Before Miles could tell him about it, Omar arrived. "Good morning, everybody, I'm glad you all could come on such a short notice. Miles, did Ralph get a chance to fly yet?"

"Not yet!" Ralph said enthusiastically. He tried to pick up the fluorescent green drone, but Katie batted his hand away.

"Not that one, Ralph, that's mine," she said.

As Ralph picked up another, Miles shook his head. "And not that one, that's my new special lady. Her name is *Raptor*. 'Cuz she's a bird of prey."

Looking at the last drone on the bench, he cocked his head at Omar. "Is this one spoken for?"

Miles nodded. "Yeah, it says Ralph on it in invisible ink."

Soon Ralph was buzzing around the course Miles had set up, zipping and bobbing easily through the hoops and gates. He gained more confidence with time, and his ability to take the hairpin turns increased.

Omar watched, amazed at how good these kids really were. Ralph came to a stop at the finish line, and Katie and Miles set up to race him around the course. It was a sight to see, each within their own quirks, each testing their drones to the fullest. Little did they know that most of the rest of the task force was watching. Miles again fought them off and won the heat, and when they were all done, they were laughing and just having fun like the teenagers they were. The spectators went back to what they were doing, shaking their heads.

Omar clapped and asked if they could get down to work. All three nodded, so he continued. "Good, let's grab a conference room and have a chat," he said, pointing across the way to a newly constructed meeting area. Once inside, they were surprised to see it was filled with maps and computers.

A young woman entered and closed the door behind her. She was dressed in a dark pants suit, wore short hair tied sharply in a tight pony tail, and she had a very direct manner. "My name is Liz Chapman. I'm project leader for this phase of Operation Sky Hawk," she announced, eying Miles, Katie, and Ralph. "I presume all of you agreed to be here, so I'll get right to it. Gang activity has become intolerable. It appears there's something on the horizon that's pretty scary. We've been working on this case for over six months, and we are concerned that these crews have increasingly turned to technology to solve some of their problems. That's why we need you three."

Nobody said a word – no jokes, no wisecracks. Miss Chapman continued. "We used to think this was more old school stuff, fist fights, turf wars, and the like. Now they have some of the most advanced weapons on the market. They can shoot someone from the sky and kill them from the comfort of their front porch."

"We've had drive-bys since I was little," Katie said.

Liz apparently didn't like the interruption, and she frowned at Katie, making her feel uncomfortable. "They're using drones to take out rivals from two miles away. It's a whole new level," she emphasized. "And they're watching from their laptops, and sharing the kill videos. Now if that doesn't frighten you..."

"What's that got to do with us?" Ralph asked. "We didn't do it."

Omar took over the presentation and walked over to a map. "Bottom line, we need your help," he said. "We're asking for your insights, your guidance. These guys aren't dumb. They've figured out how to take advantage of this new technology and we're gonna have more trouble than our glass will hold. We're lucky they're still not that smart, but they'll learn as they go. And they'll keep recruiting geeks and nerds, pardon the expression. They'll keep coming after kids like you, and for every kid with a conscience who says 'No," they'll find five more that will dive right in."

The trio stayed quiet. They liked the compliment but saw a hint of where this was going.

"Miles says you're the best of the best, because of your kick-ass flying abilities," Omar said, purposely stroking their egos. Moving closer to the map on the wall, Omar began to point. "This state map is where most of the shootings have taken place over the last four years. That's 84 pins. Eight-four dead kids. These pins with flags are shootings within the last twelve months. And these green pins are the ones suspected to be drones."

Omar decided to break some of the tension. "Well, three of those are actually claimed to be flying saucers," he deadpanned. This brought out laughter from everyone present except Miles, who always thought his Dad's jokes were lame.

"We're asking that each of you go ahead and get recruited. Go along with their program and be our eyes and ears. From here at the Command Post, you'll each have a watcher assigned to you, and you'll be protected at all times. You'll only be at risk for three months, and by then we'll have what we need. You won't have to testify in court, and you won't ever be identified in any court papers. We'll fake an arrest so you'll appear to be in just as much trouble as the homies if need be, and if it all works out, you'll be eligible for a discreet scholarship at a state university. You won't be at risk for snitching or anything like that. You'll just work it like they ask, and we'll do the rest."

He turned the meeting back over to Liz, who immediately stood up and opened the door motioning everyone to follow her. "Notice all the windows are being painted over for privacy," she pointed out. We've got extra security loaned from the FBI. We can't be bugged, hacked, or snooped on. In six months, this building will be the home of a bottled distributor, but for now it belongs to us. Nobody will wear a badge or uniform, and nobody will roll up in police cars. We'll carpool in so there isn't unusual activity, and there won't even be much light visible from here."

The tour continued. "In this room, you will find your work benches. This will be where our toys are built and repaired," she said, glancing into the room. It was full of tools, including a drill press, soldering irons, electronic testing devices, and more. It was a full-on lab for keeping them in the sky.

"If you look at those pallets against the wall, they're the latest drones on the market. We've got funding from Homeland Security to give you whatever you need, and we're one of three pilot programs across the country. Some of these are prototypes that haven't even been released yet, but the manufacturers are all-in. That goes for the headgear and transmitters as well. You've already seen the track. You'll learn to fly within our legal constraints and most important, learn how we communicate within our groups. You may wear a bug, but that will be situational and TBD."

"TBD?" Ralph repeated.

"To be determined," Liz responded. "Any questions?"

All three-looked stunned and remained silent. The full impact had not reached home yet. "Good, then before we actually begin your training, each one you must sign this agreement of confidentiality. Not to put a fine point on it, but any breach could get you shot for treason."

"Say what?" Ralph said, eyes bugging out.

"Just a joke to make sure you're listening," Liz said with a grim, forced smile.

"What happens here, stays here. Your parents will all be contacted by our team leads and will have to sign as well. Remember, this place does not exist. You are on the front lines, so no bragging on Facebook, no posting on Instagram, no tweets, no blogs." She stared at them intently.

"We will issue you burner phones for this project. They're to be used only for official business, and every conversation you make on this phone will automatically be recorded in its entirety. You will have a distress code unique to you, as well. Outside this warehouse, there will always be a work van observing and recording everyone that comes and goes near you."

Ralph seemed unimpressed. "Is there any food?" he asked.

Liz finally brightened. "Snacks are in the kitchen," she said. "Grab what you want."

The three new law enforcement agents sat down in the kitchen and wolfed down some sandwiches and trail mix and inhaled a few sodas. Katie asked for bottled water, naturally, and picked at a few raw vegetables while the boys ate until they were full. As they were cleaning up, Liz brought in a stack of three-ringed binders with training materials. "OK, study time," she commanded. For about an hour, the trio read up on known gang houses, suspected gang members, and estimates of how much weed, meth, and fentanyl the gangs were moving.

"Is there going to be a test?" Ralph asked. Miles was glad to see that Ralph's sense of humor had fully returned.

Omar came in and smiled. "Sort of. We contacted your principal and arranged to get you some class credit for participating."

Ralph and Miles exchanged glances. "More good news!" Miles said.

Finally, they'd absorbed about as much as they could for one day. They agreed to return the next afternoon after school, and once they'd cleared out, Liz and Omar picked up the notebooks and stashed them away.

"You think they actually understand how dangerous this may be?" she asked him.

"No, probably not," he admitted.

CHAPTER 16: Exposed

As Miles, Ralph and Katie huddled just inside the garage door they were met by Liz. "Morning," the business-like lady said, with a firm, no-nonsense tone. "Please follow me to the supply room."

As she entered, Miles noticed three large bins with their names above each one, printed in large bold letters. The trio opened their lockers and saw racing and recreational drones. The trio had the largest drones they have ever seen. Liz was quick to intercept them from being handled.

"That drone is for graduation" with a smile that looked more like a smirk. "Please carry the satchel that has your racing drone, headgear and transmitter and meet me at the track." Following the order, they all walked over and as they did, they noticed more individuals and equipment set up. Three adults were approaching the track with their own gear.

Liz introduced them. "This is Arlan, Kendra and Grady, your team leads," she said. Arlan was tall, dressed in light blue coveralls. About 30ish, he had a boyish smile and short, thinning blonde hair. Kendra was also wearing coveralls, but she was slimmer and younger, with a two inch cropped golden brown natural and not much of a smile, Katie guessed. Kendra did have a geeky manner that suggested they might be great friends. Grady was about the same age as Kendra, and looked like he might have just escaped the 'hood. He had been issued the same coveralls, but they looked better on him. He had an interesting scar on his arm that Miles stared at.

"This is Miles, Katie and Ralph, our newest trainee team members. They volunteered for Operation Sky Hawk, and all the paperwork is squared away. There will be plenty of time to get to know each other, so let's get the logistic issues out of the way."

Addressing everyone, Liz began. "As of today, you will be split up into three teams, and each of you will have a team lead. Because of all the activity going on in this warehouse, everyone will need to wear these ID badges at all times. Do not lose them!" she emphasized, purposely looking at the trainees. "Your badges are color-coded to identify you, your team and area restrictions within this project's confines," she continued. "You'll be with your teams today for a couple of hours, and when you are done, you'll be escorted over to the work bench area. Have a good time," she concluded, leaving abruptly.

At the race track, the trainees were told that this would be an opportunity for everyone to get to know each other and observe their flying abilities. First, the trainees all took turns flying their drones, then the team leads flew a few laps. The trainees and team leads were actually surprised at how well each individual flew. As everyone exchanged drone batteries, Grady invited them to take a breather, have something to drink and sit awhile.

"We'll all get to know one another later, but for now, how about I'll kick off and share a little something about me. I've been flying drones for about five years. I worked for Flappo Industries as a designer and developer of miniature, unmanned vehicles, both aerial and ground vehicles. Kendra, you want to go next?"

"Thanks Grady. I've been flying drones for about eight years with the US Air Force Joint Special Operations Command. I was part of a team mostly stationed overseas. I had the opportunity to fly the latest platforms, including the Predator and Reaper drones and other classified UAV's in combat situations. Pretty hectic and stressful work; sometimes you end up flying six days in a row, sometimes thirteen hours at a stretch. At the end of my tour, I didn't re-up, so I was discharged last month. There is currently a critical shortage of skilled pilots, so you might consider this profession. There's a hefty signing bonus too. That's enough of me for now, so Arlan, you want to go next?"

"Thanks, Kendra. I'm a former news media helicopter pilot. I've been flying drones on and off for about four years. However, I've been flying RC's for some fifteen years. It was a hobby of mine, flying competitively until I got married and had kids. So, my advice to the three of you is enjoy it now, before life takes over," he said with a smile.

Miles, Katie and Ralph looked at each other with amazement. It also humbled each one of them to the point of initial intimidation. "You want to go next Miles?"

"I've been flying drones for about a year or less, but I've been flying helicopters and planes for about six years. I like messing around to figure out the different things you can do with their systems and stuff like that," he added, but not wanting to share everything he'd done while pointing at Ralph to go next.

Ralph nodded. "I've been flying on and off for seven years, both helicopters and planes and now, of course, drones. As you can see I'm kind of restricted now because of my accident," he said warily.

Grady sensed Ralph was embarrassed and chimed in. "But the question is, can you fly, and do you want to fly?"

"Yeah, let's do this," Ralph nodded.

Katie just stood there so everyone could read her T-shirt that read "Watch This Space."

"I've been flying about five years with drones. I never got into helicopters or planes. The reason I like drones is for the speed, and most of all beating Miles and Ralph," she said with her usual confidence.

"We'll see about that," Miles declared while giving a high five to Ralph.

The team leads told the trainees that they were good pilots, but the real value would come when each lead had the opportunity to have individual conversations. The team leads excused themselves for a few minutes, then returned to the group. "Ok, here will be the team assignments," Grady proposed. "Arlan will take Ralph, Kendra will take Katie, and I'll take you, Miles. Here is what we're gonna do. Each of you will fly two laps and your lead will come in at any point. Your job is to keep flying regardless of what we do. Who wants to go first?"

"I'll go first," Ralph volunteered, laying his drone on the table. He took to the air and after one lap, his team lead Arlan jumped in chasing him, drafting behind, then jumping in front and quickly taking the lead. Then he'd disappear, and show up again without notice. It seemed like a big cat-and-mouse game.

Katie went next, with Kendra dropping in and out of her flight path followed by Miles and Grady. After everyone had flown, the team met and did a quick critique.

"Ok, this time the team lead will start off," Grady asserted, laying his drone down on the starting line. "Find your lead, then chase him in hot pursuit. Remember the course is not going to be this official course. The team lead will be restricted to fly in this quadrant, though."

By the time Katie had finished her turn, both Miles and Ralph were yelling aloud in encouragement. When Miles raced last, the group was fully engaged. Emotions were high, but so was the sense of team cohesion.

Once that exercise ended, the course lighting was dimmed and the process repeated itself. Finally, all three trainees were exhausted, and so were the leads. They took a short break, swapped out their batteries, and sipped on sodas.

Grady brought them over to a rectangular table that had a tarp covering its objects. Liz reappeared and peeled the tarp away with a flourish. "If I could have your attention, here is an early prototype of a weapons delivery system that was developed by one of you."

Katie and Ralph exchanged glances, and Ralph made a subtle nod towards Miles. Katie frowned and stole a glance over at Miles, who was trying to avoid her look.

Liz continued. "Look closely at this little one. You can see some arms that can protrude to attach things magnetically, such as a miniature GPS device." Miles tried to look calm; so far, he was succeeding.

Liz next pointed at the drone at the end of the table. "This one has been fitted with an AR-15 pistol that has been further modified with a suppressor, bump stock, and customized firing mechanism. It will empty a magazine with a single pull of the trigger like a machine gun." She turned to Miles.

"Did I get all that right, Miles?" She was not smiling.

Miles stammered. "Uh, shorter barrel, too," he said. Katie punched him on the arm, her way of saying she'd talk with him later.

Liz wasn't smiling. "Any questions?"

"I have one," Ralph said, raising his hand. "When do we get to shoot something?"

"Never!" Liz said emphatically. "Those drones are not for kids. Our job is to keep you out of danger, not put you right in the middle of it."

Ralph seemed disappointed.

Liz looked at her watch. "I think it's time to call it a day. Let's spend some time reading your briefing books and finish up," she commanded.

CHAPTER 17: Preparation for War

Arriving at the training center just one week after signing up, a surprise awaited them. The van that brought Ralph kept its engine running, and Katie and Miles were told to get in. The driver said the trainees were going to get a special treat. They eventually found themselves out in the country, some twenty or so miles from the command post, and as they looked out the heavily tinted windows, they soon realized they had no idea where they had been driven to.

They marveled how quiet it was, and how empty. There were hardly any people. It was like another world.

The van pulled up to a locked gate, and after the driver punched in a code, they parked in the visitor's section. While Ralph and his wheelchair were lowered to the ground, Miles and Katie took in the new sounds and smells.

"Even the birds are different," Katie said, pointing to a ring-necked pheasant clucking in a nearby corn field, searching for kernels in the wilted stalks.

In front of the van was a small building. They were led into it, instantly noticing it was far different inside. Several people were peering into computer monitors, and speaking into headsets, while others were working on equipment.

One of the technicians looked up, walked over to them, and introduced himself. "Hi, my name is Jason." They each shook his hand.

Miles eyed him carefully. Jason looked like he was a typical geeky Millennial, with large black glasses, a wispy beard, and perhaps 15-20 pounds overweight. He had a booming voice that filled the area.

"Welcome to Crosshairs," he said happily, expanding his arms to full wingspan. "This is our little city in the country. This is where we train for high altitude surveillance and tracking missions. We have had at least one drone in the air at all times for the last three weeks. We're building a tracking database of the key vehicles the gangs are using, logging their stops, and tracking their moves."

Ralph whistled. "I know this is our tax dollars at work, but this ain't city stuff. You guys must be feds."

Jason smiled and nodded. "Yep, Homeland Security and FBI joint task force. Hang tight; your team leads will be here in a few minutes, so feel free to step outside and look around, but don't touch anything. The sentry droids might get activated and blast you with their lasers."

Katie was startled. "Seriously?" she asked.

"Nah, just kidding. Gotta dream big," he said with a smile, then turned to talk to one of the technicians staring at a monitor.

They walked outside and looked around. The little seven-acre village was like a Hollywood movie set. There were fake buildings, trees, roads and mannequins everywhere - some sitting, some jogging, and others gathered in groups. There were even cars and trucks on the roads and parked next to the curbs. Walking around briefly the trio actually felt they were in a movie set, as everything seemed so real. There were cameras everywhere they looked, on buildings, poles, even on top of a truck with what looked like a radar dish.

About that time, the team leads drove up in a large, brown boxy truck and got out. "Morning ya'll," Kendra said. "Pretty cool stuff, huh? Let's get busy!" The trio followed their leads to the back of the truck and lent a hand unloading the gear.

"As always, we'll work in teams. Everyone will get to fly the entire course, so take a look at the map. We'll play 'follow the leader' and work on some chase scenarios in an open environment.

Bur first, let's move inside. I want to keep you all separated, so split up into individual rooms."

Within a few minutes, the first drones were buzzing around the compound in hot pursuit. First at low altitude, then higher, the drones whizzed around the entire city. Soon, all six were in the air at once, but eventually, each craft had to land and get a new battery. For at least an hour, they kept at it, dodging each other, landing for another battery, and getting back into the "battle." Finally, Miles came to a rest without another battery pack to pop in. He followed his lead into the monitoring area.

He was surprised to learn that the leads were all being directed from the monitors, following instructions issued by the seated technicians. Miles was the first trainee into the room, and he marveled at how the techs were able to monitor the entire situation from their view.

Katie followed and quietly watched as well. Then Ralph wheeled in. Jason hit a few keys and soon, they were reviewing the video capture of their training session.

Suddenly, Miles brightened. "Wait, now I get it. You weren't training us; you were training the rest of your team," he said triumphantly.

Jason nodded. "Yep, you guys are ready. But the rest of us need to catch up. Plus, we wanted to see what you do under pressure and get an idea of your patterns, your go-to moves. We can log all this and feed it into the system, and hopefully, we can identify you just based on how your drone is moving."

The trio smiled at each other. "Can you help Katie fix her tendency to stay soft on the left?" Ralph asked.

Katie punched him, while Jason ignored the banter. "In five days, we'll be doing all this for real. We don't know what kind of situation you're going to be in. You may have to pretend to let one of us catch you making a run. You may have to pretend to get away."

Katie objected. "Pretend? Have any of you old geezers caught any of us yet?"

Jason laughed. "Don't get cocky. Look, everyone. You've been trained well. You all know how to fly fast, and we think you're ready to fly safely and in accordance with this mission. You know our equipment and you know our patterns. There isn't any obstacle that you haven't been able to fly against. You're some kick-ass pilots," he admitted.

The last exercise the trainees participated in was as close to a "live fire" scenario as they were going to get. Liz explained the challenge. "This time, there will be friendly drones and enemy drones. Each team will be on their own frequency and hear a lot more chatter. The object will be to pursue and shoot down your opposing team," Liz said.

"Shoot them down?" Ralph echoed, excitedly.

Liz shook her head. "No, you don't get to actually shoot, but if you can get within three meters, your transmitter will automatically vibrate, letting you know you're locked on. When that happens, you can press the bright red button and your drone will send out a signal that will interfere with the drone's radio frequency and log as a kill. Basically, you fry its motors, causing it to crash.".

"Wow," the trio said in unison.

"No names in this scenario. Miles, you're T1. Katie, you're T2. Ralph, you're T3. Arlan, Grady and Kendra, you're L1, L2, and L3. OK, gear up."

As the trainees and leads set up their headgear and prepped their drones, Liz pre-positioned a vanload of new visitors behind a transparent, bullet-proof room so they'd have both a physical viewing area and a view from enlarged monitors. Miles had never seen them before; he figured they were higher-up feds.

"Ok, everyone to your stations!" she ordered over the loudspeaker.

Miles heard himself starting to hum his favorite pre-race song. "Quiet on the mic, T1," he heard.

Then, through the headsets, the pilots all heard the magic word: "Launch!"

What happened next was a true aerial spectacle. Drones were flying everywhere, with commands constantly coming through the headsets. Miles was piloting his drone when he received a message to proceed to the far, east side of Crosshairs. He was already being chased by one of the leads, but he broke free and zipped over. Once there, he noticed a drone holding some fifty feet off the ground.

"T1 to base. Permission to engage," he said mechanically.

"Go ahead T1." But before he could lock on, the drone shot skyward. Miles took off after it in hot pursuit. Soon, he was closing, and he could tell by the moves he was seeing in front of him that it was Kendra; she tended to drive high and to the right when she was stressed. He got closer, and he lifted the cover on his firing mechanism, engaging the seeking circuits. His transmitter began to vibrate, but before he could fire, the drone dove steeply.

Miles followed in hot pursuit once again. This time he closed in more prepared, and finally got into position. He pushed the red button. The enemy drone started to wobble then before his eyes it lost momentum and started smoking, then fell to the ground.

"T1, back to base," he heard in his ear.

Miles was shocked to realize he was the last trainee to return. Both Katie and Ralph were already done, goggles off. They smiled. "Took you long enough," Katie said.

"Is it Miller Time?" he asked, even though he was nowhere near old enough to buy beer.

Before Katie could answer, Liz herded them all into the monitor room. Jason pulled up Katie's aerial combat video and Miles watched as it took off in hot pursuit of a blazing red drone. Soon, the enemy drone turned on her and pursued *her*. She evaded that drone by dropping altitude and slowing down, then completing a 360-degree spiral. The enemy drone flew past her, and she turned to pursue and caught quickly, sending it to the ground.

They watched his maneuvers next, and he was pretty proud of himself, watching his own moves.

Then Ralph was up, and Miles watched closely as his friend chose to go high to improve his view. Ralph spotted an enemy drone down the street, then circled from the left side and closed in. He must have already engaged the firing mechanism, because when enemy drone showed itself, he was already set to fire. That drone also settled meekly into the ground.

Jason clicked across his screen with the mouse and brought up a different view of the same action. It was harder to follow from a bird's eye view, even on the large screens. But it better showed the frenzy of so much activity, how hectic everything can appear to the controllers back at base.

On the van ride back to the city, Katie moved to sit near Miles. "So, what's up with you humming *Pushing Mach 5* every time we fly?" she asked.

"It calms my nerves," he responded defensively.

She rolled her eyes.

CHAPTER 18: Infiltration

Bubba Brew was a new microbrewery situated a few blocks from where Miles lived. The owners had volunteered to host the next drone tournament in town, and it was finally happening on the next weekend. No pre-qualification entry rules were going to be established, which allowed for anyone to enter.

On the Monday following their big "Crosshairs" session, Omar called a meeting of the six in preparation for the upcoming tourney. He was all set with a presentation, so he could flash images on the wall-mounted screen behind him.

"We're confident that our favorite gang bangers will be at this event," he said, with photos of several known gang members.

"This is just the thing we've been waiting for. A two-day, open event, sure to generate some buzz. Your entry fees have already been paid, and you'll get the chance to fly your personal drones, using the newest Ocular Observer headgear." He advanced his slide show to a picture of the new gear.

"We modified their appearances so they don't look too good, though. We don't want to tip our hand."

Miles exchanged glances with Ralph. They snickered like schoolboys hatching a prank. "Ringer!" Ralph whispered, but not quietly enough.

"Boys!" Omar said sharply. "Don't let the headgear out of your sight, please. They are designed to look just like everyone else's equipment, but they are far, far better."

"Now, the real point of all this is to get you recruited. Your team leads will skip the flying and just show up as spectators. They'll always be within listening range, so if you get approached, all you have to do is crunch your toes in your shoes, and it'll automatically send out an alert and begin tracking."

He advanced and showed them a picture of the tiny devices that fit into their shoes. "Just don't turn it off."

The trio sat alertly, which he appreciated. "Ok, Katie, what will you do if one of them comes up to you?"

Katie smiled. "I'll play hard to get, but eventually I'll cave and agree to join."

"How about you, Miles?"

"Me? I'm the cocky type, right? The bad ass. I agree on the spot, ready for the challenge," he added with a grin.

"Ralph?"

"I'm going to sit this one out, so we don't all join up at once. I'm going to act interested, if they even ask me. Mostly just hang out taking in the sights, taking accidental pictures of the creeps with selfies or something."

On the first day of the tournament, there must have been 300 people scattered around the venue, with at least 50 pilots. Miles had seen most of them before, but there were a few new faces. He didn't see anyone to worry about, and as he watched the drones being unpacked that he would have to go against, he felt even better. None of them looked like they could match his gear.

The sponsors were able rent the old Dynacrypt manufacturing plant for the event. It was the perfect site for the race. It had 100,000 square foot of space, column-free, with thirty-foot ceilings. The course design was elongated with straight lanes, a couple of hairpin turns, some slalom turns, several dramatic changes in elevation, and a few gates to go up and over, through or even under.

There was the main track, an area for the pit row, and track sides for pilots preparing for their individual races. The course was netted entirely, protecting spectators from any errant drones that could hurt someone from the temporary, elevated bleachers.

There would be categories for single drones, teams, and freestyle. Each three-lap race which would last anywhere from four to five minutes each.

Finally, the emcee got things rolling. It was an older gentleman with a smooth, deep voice, dressed in a kind of faux tuxedo. "Welcome, everyone!" he practically shouted. His voice echoed through the building, and his face was visible on several monitors strategically placed.

"If I may have your attention, please. Before we start racing today, we have a special treat for you. As you may have noticed as you entered the hall today there were nets sprawled out everywhere, here in the arena and alongside the corridors. First of all, they serve as a safety net to prevent anyone from getting hit by a drone. Second, they act as a barrier, so please be respectful and don't cross into those areas. We have some exciting pilots here today represented by seven drone racing clubs from around the country. At registration, today we arbitrarily picked a pilot from each team who have agreed to fly an exhibition to show everyone what drone racing is all about and to get things started. These pilots will fly this designated course three times and then we'll announce the first race."

As the event emcee called the pilots to place their drones on the starting line, Katie raised her hand and stopped the process. She walked over to Ralph, gave him her drone, the transmitter and goggles. "Here you fly, no free lunch for you." She encouraged him with a slap on the shoulders. Ralph was beaming as he rolled his chair over to the starting line with the crowd yelling and clapping for inspiration.

As the pilots huddled around the event emcee they were given instructions about the course then they headed to the middle of the arena and waived to the crowd that brought a thunderous yell. "Ladies and gentlemen please bring your attention to the center of the arena and those of you that cannot see look at the nearest monitor. We're going to dim down the lights around the flying course to illuminate the drones. ARE YOU READY" he shouted.

"ARE YOU READY? Five, four, three, two, one, GO" he yelled. The drones rose from the floor and quickly exited the room through a double-wide door. Turning left, they hugged the wall racing about forty yards to an escalator flying up a level still hugging the circular hallway.

Continuing on, they reached the far end and flew down a flight of stairs. There was another escalator, followed by another escalator, and as the pilots reached the open area they shot up straight towards the ceiling about ninety feet whereby they immediately did a hairpin turn. This brought applause and clapping. Immediately, the drones dove downward to the floor, flying under an overhead walkway screaming by at seventy miles per hour.

Retracing their route, they reentered the arena and everyone was standing and yelling. Anyone who had never seen drone racing before was in for a treat. Two more times the pilots flew around the arena and when it was over, the crowd roared.

Ralph was so elated he spun his wheelchair in a 360, which brought another roar from the crowd. "Now that's what I call excitement!" the event emcee told the crowd.

During the break, Ralph had no trouble picking out the "recruiters" they were expecting. This time there were four of them, with tattoos and baggy jeans. The recruiters split up in two-man teams and began prowling. Ralph snapped a few pictures, pretending to be taking pictures of the banners flying above them. He then wheeled his chair around the arena and saw a few more people talking to pilots and while observing them saw they were given business cards. He took pictures of that as well.

Katie was surrounded by bystanders who wanted her autograph. Apparently, she had won her initial race. Her team lead Kendra stood vigilantly by. On the other side of the arena Miles was in a discussion with someone that seemed to perturb him. Wheeling near him you could hear him bragging about his chances and his equipment. Other contestants didn't appreciate him and were voicing their opinions about who was going to be the best.

Over the loud speaker Katie's final race was being announced so Ralph wheeled as close as he could and pushed himself in-between some fans that turned out to have taken an interest in her flying abilities.

Ralph thought this was his best chance so he started chatting small talk with them. "I used to race against that gal and she whipped us almost every time. She knows most of the local pilots and has a pretty good reputation. Most of the guys try to hit on her and she loves to party," he added. "You can easily identify her because she always wears those T-shirts bragging about how good she is," he continued with emphasis.

"Do you still fly?" the one wearing a hoodie whispered as he of turned to Ralph and looked down at his wheel chair.

Bothered by his remarks, Ralph raised his voice. "Look dude, I'm crippled from my waist down not my hands or arms. Besides, I can fly enough to kick all your asses," he retorted with an attitude. "You must be blind. I just flew, and if you'd had taken your head out of your ass you would have seen me," he said with disdain.

Because of the attention around them, the small group apologized, turned and walked away. As they did Ralph's team lead snapped a picture and then looked at Ralph as if to say don't overdo it.

Besides the exhibition, the freestyle was the best of the day's event and had the most people watching. It was so amazing to watch pilots on a prescribed course do flips, rolls, nose dives, flying backwards, and even speed trials.

By Sunday, the word had gotten out about the drone event and carloads of people showed up, making it practically impossible to find parking. Transit busses began to transport people from park N rides. Even school busses were brought out to assist.

There was so much activity it was difficult to see which event to view. There was no age limitation and every age was well represented. Seems like every race and gender were competing and for a while it looked like the United Nations team.

Manufacturers were represented and were selling all types of drones to the public. No one was allowed to fly their newly-purchased drones on the property, but there were stations where anyone was given an opportunity to take off and land within a small, netted area.

When the tournament was officially over, it seemed like nobody wanted to go home. The emcee kept reminding people where the exits were, but people seemed to want to linger. The event was a huge success, and the local newspapers' headlines read, "Drone Races Thrill Crowds."

CHAPTER 19: Used

The following week both Katie and Miles reported that they had agreed to join the BBB Drone Club. They conveyed the process to Omar declaring that the club wanted to know how well the new recruits flew so they both agreed to fly innocently around the neighborhood. The decision was that there was no need to have the team leads nearby as to the perceived innocence of the event and where the flying would take place. Miles interjected and stated they were told to make sure they had their SD cards because they would be flying a course designed by them. Showing up near a vacant field they were met with a couple of club members who changed their minds and said we were to fly a different course. They pointed out a course located about ten blocks from Ralph's house which inadvertently took them over an industrial site filled with parked semi's, buildings and surrounded by what looked like a high security fence. The goal was to fly at a high altitude over the vacant field, film a 360 of the area, swoop down and fly the fence line, around a point, then shoot back over the distribution center. Upon returning to their take off area, both Katie and Miles were told they both were damn good pilots. They were then asked how long their drones could stay airborne, what kind of tricks they could do and do they like taking pictures in which both shook their head with approval. When they were all done flying they were asked to give up their SD cards so that they could take them back to the club's president to view their piloting skills.

Katie on the way back home with Miles just laughed aloud. "That was the easiest flying I've done for a long time and it really didn't take that much skill. Hell, anyone could have flown that course and that's a fact."

"Yeah I know and it just goes to show you that these guys don't know what the heck they're doing. Even my little bro Kenny could have flown that course," Miles added.

Later that evening Omar asked how it went and Miles just shrugged. "It was crazy dad. All they wanted to know is if we could fly in a straight line, go up, turn around, and come back without hitting anything. Guess it was a test to see if we could really fly, so we'll see what they're up to next time they ask us to do something. Funny thing is they all watched us compete in the tourney a few weeks ago so whatever." With that Miles shrugged his shoulder saying he was going to go upstairs and call Ralph.

Within a few days Omar was called into a briefing by the task force commander who was agitated from the beginning and pacing back and forth as everyone was getting seated. "Hurry the hell up, I've got a lot to cover today" he bellowed irritably. "I'll turn the meeting over to Mr. Samuel Schultz after I get everyone up to speed with the latest burglaries. Two days ago, the X-Fox distribution warehouse was hit. It seems like it was an inside job because someone knew exactly what time the semis would arrive and unload their contents because they were in and out without anyone knowing. Unfortunately, the security guard was shot and killed by what appears to be the fleeing vehicle. The guard was shot attempting to chase down the vehicle on foot instead of calling it in. Anyway, the contents taken from a parked semi were the latest and most expensive RC drones whatever the hell that means."

"Remote control vehicles" Omar bellowed out flaunting his limited knowledge.

"They must have had multiple people because of the amount of equipment stolen it would have taken them a couple of hours, but it sounds like it was all done in fifteen minutes or so, before guard change," he continued.

"How many drones were taken?" another spoke out.

Mr. Schultz given the nod to respond said that five or six full pallets were taken. "We're still comparing our order to the actual shipping and receiving documents. For some reason, there were so many people going over the scattered area that we'll need computer confirmation of the exact total. However, I'd estimate that between 100-200 drones were stolen."

"Hell, that's enough to start a war," a colleague blurted out.

"Well, we better hope not," the commander responded. "Ok Mr. Schultz, the floor is all yours."

"Good afternoon everyone, like your commander just said we were hit pretty hard a few days ago. There's been an uptake in burglaries over the past six or seven months or so. The culprits seem to be pretty sophisticated and well organized. It appears as though the new fad is consumer electronic toys. Because of the new craze it'll be easy to find a fence to offload these drones. They've been hitting industrial parks primarily with distribution facilities. It's as though someone is surveilling our sites, monitoring shipping and knowing what specific trucks to hit. There used to be a time when the driver would leave his truck and someone would hot wire it and take it. We put a stop to thieves taking our trucks to an offsite area, monitoring to see if they had GPS systems which automatically triggered the police. Thieves used to disengage the cab from the trailers but we started installing king pin locks that prevented the tractor and trailer from being separated. No alarms went off on this heist that would have triggered the devices if the driver had gone off route because it happened in our own delivery yard. No one tried to drive the semi away because if they had, it would have been immobilized because the driver had triggered the lock down device and turned it in with the key. On this particular trailer, there was no door intrusion locks which would have shown any tampering. We're still looking into this because that should have been standard practice. What we do know is that there was a lot of noise that evening as the construction company was doing some concrete drilling to repair some ramps due to a runaway truck last week. The noise would have seemed normal and would have probably drowned out any other normal noise. A fork lift was used to transfer the pallets from the trailer to another truck and like I said it all happened very quickly and the only witness ended up losing his life, so we'll never know who or what he saw. We were informed that an empty truck was located, but it's being processed so we don't know if that was the truck used to burglarize our shipments. That's all I have so if there are any questions I'll answer the best that I can for now" Mr. Schultz somberly reported.

"You mentioned that there has been an uptake in these burglaries, so what about the other ones, how were they done?" one of the task force members inquired.

"A few months ago, entry was made by sawing into the fiberglass ceiling panel in the trailer and they were able to cut into the aluminum joists. The skin on these trailer roofs are rather thin sheets of aluminum supported by galvanized steel beam sections, so practically anybody with good cutting tools could gain entry pretty quickly. Same thing about what was taken however, there were no deaths or injuries. What we're noticing is that companies don't want to report their losses because it's bad for their business to get the word out that they can't be relied upon to deliver goods. Also, they'd rather eat the cost than to report to their insurance companies. So, this data in not very comprehensive and as a national business we're looking at ways to shut down these criminals. That's why we had the docks being repaired at night. We're do to get large shipments by weeks end and if we can't support those shipments they'd take their business elsewhere. Otherwise we wouldn't have been doing that dock repair at night" he related while taking his seat.

"Thank you, Mr. Schultz quite revealing. Any more questions from anyone?" the chief asked while looking down at some documents. "In checking at our data base, the underground is buzzing with bidding wars. Apparently drone pilots are selling their services to do surveillance on homes for burglaries by taking video and photographs identifying weak security spots such as French doors, patio glass doors, roaming dogs and neighbors. Now check this out. They are even using you know, that street view map that's linked to satellites to scan potential sites. Now if that doesn't beat all. We're up against a new breed of gangsters and we had better get up to speed to meet fire with fire, before we all become victimized. With the five million or so of these flying robot drones expected for market this year they estimate eighteen million of them will be on the market by 2020."

CHAPTER 20: The Sky Is Humming

Katie, Miles and Ralph caught up to each other one day in the park during what were essentially basic flying lessons. Each of them had three BBB member trainees learning how to fly. The sound of electric humming came from multiple drones flying haphazardly across the sky, with no predetermined pattern.

The trainees appeared to be enjoying flying, with intermittent whoops and catcalls as they survived close calls and avoided each other. Periodically a drone would take off across the soccer field, swoop down, and then fly off in raggedy patterns, revealing the inexperience of the trainees. Their lack of experience was more than made up for with enthusiasm, however, and over time, their confidence grew.

Miles watched it all with a crooked smile. He glanced at Katie and hollered out, "What ya got going over there? Seems that your students are having trouble flying a straight line," he teased.

"How many drones did your trainees break today?" Katie answered back, equally amused.

Ralph chimed in. "It's time to see how much your students have learned. Let's have some fun. How about a short race, your trainees against mine?"

Within minutes Miles, Ralph and Katie briefly got together then with the nine student pilots and decided to have an impromptu race. A course was set up and the trio flew it first to show them what it was going to be like. Each trainee would take two laps, then the next one would go. At the end, the instructors would take a two-lap turn.

The students had a hard time staying on course. A few of them swerved off but got back on track with some serious taunting. One of the students got so excited that he flew his drone right into the soccer net, seemingly without even attempting to turn. Another got cocky and tried to take a hairpin turn at full speed, but ended up flying his drone into a tree with a loud bang. Drone fragments showered the ground.

Katie's team took first place, and they all strutted around giving each other high five's and bragging to each other. Katie insisted on forcing the trainees to clean up their debris, and when the park was more or less respectable again, the teams and trainers went their separate ways.

Omar called a meeting with the trio to check in and to see what their groups were doing. The trio didn't have anything much to say other than the trainees would never place in any upcoming tournaments because they didn't have the patience to fly with good technique. Ralph explained that one of the trainees once threw his transmitter to the ground in disgust while his drone was still airborne.

"Dude was just, like 'Whatever, we got more,' and seemed pretty calm about wrecking a $500 piece of equipment," Miles reported.

Omar stroked his chin thoughtfully. "They just have some deep pockets," he decided.

"That's what I thought. But then AJ rolled up to the park and he was pissed. He rolled down his window and called this dude over to chew his ass. I don't know what he said, but when the homie came back he had a shocked look on his face, and he took things a lot more serious."

Katie agreed. "Pretty smart of AJ to check in. I noticed that we seemed to be going through drones like crazy because of all the crashes and the bent-up blades. They didn't seem to care because they'd just show up with new ones. But lately they got a little more serious and stopped going kamikaze on each other."

Omar thought about mentioning the most recent burglaries, but decided against it. "Well, keep sharp out there. Eyes and ears open at all times!" he added.

Before long, AJ's people were flying drones not only in the park, but up and down the streets. Miles saw that many of these rookies had no business flying above a crowded street, as they took too many unnecessary chances. He wondered how many of these newcomers were actually gang bangers, so he snapped a few pictures with his phone. Ralph was doing the same thing with his hidden camera, and they turned in the photos to Omar at their next meeting.

There was a local one-day tourney sponsored by Bryce's Hobby Store. This was a new hobby store just opened with hopes of getting strictly into the drone market. The purpose of the event was to show off beginner and intermediate drone types, get kids excited about flying, and to have some fun races. Unfortunately, it didn't get off on time and people were getting frustrated. When it did, people started pushing to get in line to try out drones, arguing over those taking too long or those that wanted to go next.

Some older kids even tried to take transmitters from younger kids, but oftentimes their parents kept that from happening while enjoying their kids learning to fly. Then there was a short course whereby pilots could fly at least two laps. As evening drew closer, attendees had settled down and it appeared that most of the people were having fun. Katie, Ralph and Miles really worked the crowd hard to keep the day's activities entertaining and making sure everyone who participated had fun, but it seemed that hotheads prevailed.

As the event began to close down, the owner of Bryce's Hobby Store unveiled a large crate that had been brought in and got on a bullhorn and asked if everyone had had fun. There was a deafening applause. "Thank you for your support for this event and for this recognition I have a gift for each and every one of you. At first attendees started to just walk away because usually gifts were so token that only the little kids wanted them, but as people began to see what was happening those that hadn't already left stood in line for their gift.

As it so happened, he and his helpers were giving out micro drones about the size of your palm and the transmitter also could fit in your palm. He again got on the bullhorn to announce they needed to be charged so absolutely NO flying, as the event was now closed. Those who were still waiting for their gifts and those that already had received them gave a grand applause.

Outside in the parking lot there was a commotion and from what Ralph had seen two individuals, the same ones that inside had gotten into an argument, were up in each other's faces pointing at one another and just edging to fight when all of a sudden there was a scream.

As he was being pushed up into his van, Miles started recording a video. When he looked back over his shoulder he saw the crowd began to scatter, save for one struggling individual who was bent over reaching out for help. The young man then collapsed to the ground.

Arlan finished pushing him into the van, while closing the door and told him to wait there immediately took off to aid the fallen individual. By the time he arrived the victim's eyes were open and he was motionless. Arlan attempted to do CPR but to no avail but he kept it up as until an ambulance arrived and the EMT's had taken over. Looking around everyone had disappeared and only the curious had come up to find out what had happened but there were no witnesses to this yet again useless gang killing.

Inside the van on the way home, Ralph and Miles compared notes. "What a mess," he finally said.

"Fighting over a mini-drone. Can you believe it?" Miles said, shaking his head.

"Life is cheap in the 'hood," Ralph agreed.

Arlan looked into the rear-view mirror. "Did you take any pictures tonight?"

Miles spoke up. "Yeah, I took a video. I can upload it when I get home."

The team stayed silent, lost in thought, as Arlan pulled up to Ralph's house and helped him roll up the ramp to his door.

CHAPTER 21: Sinister Drones

It didn't take long for the news to get out that there was a stabbing at the weekend's drone event. The streets were echoing revenge for the perpetrator, and trouble was brewing.

At the Sunday morning meeting, the trio discussed the drone event and the unfortunate killing. Arlan turned on the flat screen and went through the pictures that Ralph had taken and the video Miles recorded. They picked out a few faces and assigned some names, identifying individuals who possibly were involved in the arguments and fight after the event.

Then there was a discussion about how gangs will take revenge when one of their own has been attacked. Katie spoke up, saying "I had heard someone in the crowd say they wished they could fly a drone right up to that killer and blast him. Maybe it was just trash talk, because the guy was holding up a little tiny micro drone he had gotten at the event. People just laughed at him."

Ralph and Miles snickered, too. "That would be like a gnat annoying an elephant," Ralph said.

"That's what I thought, except for this one guy who never smiles pulled his cell phone out of his pocket and walked away jabbering."

"Do you know his name, or can you identify him from the pictures that we've taken so far?" the team lead asks.

"I dunno his name. He had a big orange blot on his head, though. That should narrow it down, maybe," was Katie's response.

Miles jumped up. "That's Corncob," he said. "He's the only dude I know with a big blob of bleach in his 'fro."

Omar then called the three team leads into a huddle and for a few minutes they whispered amongst themselves. There was some nodding, and then they came back into the group and decided to share some information.

"A few weeks ago, there was a burglary and between 100-200 very expensive drones were hijacked from the distributor plant across down. Our leads have not come up with anything yet but we believe that somehow whoever did this will slip up and that'll be that. It had to be an inside professional job and sooner or later something will come up." Looking at the map he pointed out the warehouse that was robbed.

Miles began to stare at the area being pointed to on the map and he immediately turned to Katie with panic on his face then back at his dad. "Remember a couple of weeks ago I told you that Katie and I had to show them how good we could fly and that it was kind of stupid? They took us to this open field where we showed them our stuff and they said to fly high over this area, hold altitude do a 360 then fly up and down this fence line and to video as we flew."

Katie nodded. "Yeah, we just freestyled around, buzzing back and forth. We even flew as close as we could to the fence without hitting the barbed wire," she added.

"Yeah, and I had to fly over a couple of fields away from where you did and around some old buildings. I remember the drone that I flew was different from the one you had. I heard someone say something like a heat sensor was attached to test the rotors, but I figured they didn't know what they were talking about. I just flew like I was told."

"We were complimented on how well we piloted those drones and were asked to give them our SD cards so they could take them back to the club's president. We were told we were the best pilots in the club and that we'd be used for more test flying, whatever that meant," Miles recalled.

Omar stood up. "That wasn't innocent flying – they were casing the property. I'm guessing they had enough information to map out the guards and track their movements. Huh," he said to himself. "Pretty smart, I gotta admit."

He excused them with a final safety message and gathered his team for a brainstorming session.

Liz walked to the front of the group. "We received a tip that these two rival gangs, the Alley Hogs and the Hood Rats had called a truce and were called to a meeting with one of our known drug lords. They were approached with a business deal. It supposedly dealt with the delivery of drugs and a plan to do surveillance for future robberies using drones. These damn things are going to be more dangerous than drive bys."

The drug lord has made a statement that "to the victor goes the spoils." Our information received stated huge quantities of drugs are being gathered and stockpiled and getting ready for distribution. Thus, the uptake in clubs, rather gangs under the guise of drone racing. Everyone is wanting to get in on this business. You can rest assured that is why Katie, Miles and Ralph are so essential to fly for these jokers. Also, notice the hobby stores being robbed and shipments being intercepted, the only craft being taken are expensive drones. It hasn't been proven but we think the drug lord is supplying the drones and testing them to see who will actually end up working for him. That's why it's so important to continue to use these kids and we need to make sure we put an invisible net around them at all times." With that he took his seat in the back of the room.

Omar thought out loud. "If history repeats itself, these two gangs are going to square off and attempt to eliminate the competition because this drone business is going to be too big not to."

As the group took in this latest information Liz stood up and walked to the front of the group past the computers, chalkboards and pictures that were pasted on the wall. "So now you know how manipulative these gangs are and how easily it is to deceive naive kids to join their groups," she said, getting straight to the point. "I think it's time to pull these kids off and increase our surveillance on the individuals already identified, and hope they'll lead us into the rat's den," she continued. "This is going to get ugly really quick, and if we don't get on top of this like yesterday, we're gonna have a war on our hands."

Looking around at the group, one of the new members stood up and walked over to the map. He turned and drew a large circle around something that hadn't been discussed. "This area was used for another crime. We believe the drone that Katie flew had a heat sensor on it and it picked up the hydroponic heat from the lights. It was a marijuana farm right under our eyes. The drone was used to scout the area and then the gang went right in took the product and attempted to extort the growers but it ended up in a shoot-out. We also got news the other day that a high-flying drone had dropped off a pistol and some drugs across the state on a prison yard without being seen by the guards, but one of our plants in the yard just happened to see it. The balls to do something like that..." he trailed off.

Then he turned around and stared at Omar. "I know you have a son who's right in the middle of this mess, but I want to take exception to what you've said, Liz. These kids are important. Why not continue and let them stay involved, because AJ is starting to take them into his confidence."

Omar thought for a minute then responded. "It's a tough call. We need more information, but I hate to put my kid, or any of these kids, in jeopardy."

Liz agreed. "Ok, then let's go over what we know so far, what we believe are going to be their next steps, and if the decision is to keep the kids on board, what role they can play and not be at risk," Liz said. It was several hours until the meeting finally broke up.

CHAPTER 22: Taken

One day, Miles had just said good-bye to Katie and was about to pedal home when fellow club member Larry Wakefield showed up. "Hey Katie, nice T-shirt," Larry said, glancing at Katie' shirt. It read FLY WITH ME. Larry was a skinny, athletic kid about Miles' age, and they'd known each other awhile. Larry wanted to know if they would like to hang out, but Katie declined, saying she had something else to do and left.

Larry apologized for not being at any of the recent club activities but said he had family issues going on. "Have you noticed all the kids flying drones now in the parks and up and down the sidewalks? All ages, too, because I saw this ole man flying an airplane and everyone was laughing at him because he was cussin' up a storm. Those free micro's given out the other week sure did start a craze."

"That's for sure, Larry, the future is here and the skies are filling up," Miles responded

"Sure was cold when Terrence was killed after the drone tourney a couple of weeks ago. Everyone knew he was a hot head but they shouldn't have killed him. They'll get what's coming to them someday, that's for sure."

"What does that mean?"

"I'd like to take a drone and fly it right into their ride, or better yet attach a gun and track them down and blast them to hell that's what I'd like to do" with emphasis.

Miles didn't respond as he just nodded with uncertainty.

"Do you think you could attach a gun to a drone?"

Being coy, Miles turned away and responded. "I suppose. Anything's possible."

"But if you could, would you, if one of your family members were shot or killed?"

"I dunno, maybe I could."

"Hey, you want to get some ice cream down the street at Hansen's? It's hot as hell out here and I'll buy."

"Sure, that sounds great, but then I need to get home."

On the way, Larry said he needed to pick something up at a friend's house and asked Miles if it was ok as he'd only be a minute. Approaching the house, Larry said they should park their bikes around the back because his parents didn't like the clutter in their front yard. Larry knocked on the back door, and an individual answered with a gruff voice and only cracked the door wide enough to see who was there. Recognizing Larry, he opened wide enough for he and Miles to enter but he kept his eyes on Miles. "Hey little bro, how's it going?" he said continuing to stare at Miles.

"It's all good. This is my friend I was talking to you about. His name is Miles."

Miles just nodded and was beginning to feel a bit uncomfortable as they were led into a different room that was dimly lit and had a few individuals standing around a table. The house smelled of body odor, old food, and dirty socks, he thought – worse than his own room, he realized. "Hey ya'll, this is my friend that I've been telling you about. Come take a look at this, Miles," Larry said, encouraging him to get closer.

What Miles saw terrified him, but he pretended to be cool. "A drone with a rifle on it? Do you plan on flying this thing? I'm sure it'll weigh too much to even get off the ground," he declared confidently.

"We figured out how to attach it, but we don't know how to trigger it remotely." One of the guys at the table rang out. "It would be nice if we could shoot this thing as fast as we needed. Kind of like a machine gun," he continued.

Miles glanced at the way he and Larry had come in and saw that his passage was blocked by some scary huge dude, wearing dark shades and crossing his arms with one of his hands gripping a pistol. Turning his attention back at the table he saw exactly what they had not done but attempted to keep it to himself. "I dunno, seems like it could be done, but I don't know how to do it," he whined in an attempt to throw them off.

Immediately one of the other guys got in Larry's face. "I thought you told us this dude could do that kind of stuff!"

"He can," Larry demanded. "Come on Miles, I know you can do it. I saw you shooting a few months ago over at the quarry. You were firing your gun from your drone and I know it sounded just like a machine gun. Right?"

"Where's it at?" an impatient bystander shouted moving closer to Miles.

"I dunno, the cops took it from me and never gave it back," Miles pleaded.

"We'll see about that. He's not leaving here until he can show us how to build one of those things, and that's a fact. We got to get this thing cause them damn dawgs done killed one of ours and we need to take care of them. We bought all them damn drones plus we got enough guns as well."

But before he could say anything else he was told to shut the hell up in no uncertain terms. By this time Miles was so scared he began to shake and wanted to cry, but all he could do was to stare at Larry then back at the drone wondering why he told on him.

At that time, an individual came in and everyone moved out of his way, obviously someone of importance. He wore very dark shades, dressed somewhat better than the rest, had lots of gold chains hanging off his neck and clean shaven. His dreads flowed back and forth getting in his way and he swatted them out of his face while staring at Miles. Looking around the room slowly his eyes met Larry's and Miles. "Who's the smart ass that knows how to get this thing done?" he demanded.

All eyes shifted to Miles, who quickly turned away from fright. "Don't act like you don't know me. You also know I can fly better than you'll ever know." With a smile, he moved closer to the table. Recognizing Miles, he said, "I know you! This is the little shit, the one from the park, aren't you?" he said looking around at everyone. So, you're that so-so called pilot flying these helicopters and airplanes doing pretty basic maneuvers. The flat spin, hell anyone could that. The falling leaf you almost got it down but it needs practice. You are looking at me like you don't know what I'm talking about. I'll explain it in terms you'll understand" he demanded while looking around the room. "It's basically a rudder stall resembling a leaf falling from a tree, but enough of this bullshit" glaring straight into Miles eyes. We still have some unfinished business, don't we? Little man, talk to me about this drone not the name brand, hell I can read. I want to know what you know."

"Well," then he hesitated thinking this was one of the hijacked drones he was told about, a few weeks ago.

"Well, what?" AJ said with an agitated raised voice.

"Ah, it's one of those expensive tricked out drones." Moving closer he began. "It's got a 6 axis Gyro, looks like a 720 HD camera which will give you about 120-degree wide angle, probably can shoot, I mean take 4k video. This is where the HD card is, looks like at least three or four pounds. It won't fly with this heavy of a rifle on it." Everyone looked at Miles and those that heard this definitely knew he was the one and knew his stuff.

"You seem to know what you're talking about. You have a photographic mind?"

"That's what I've been told. I just remember little things, that's all."

"Ok then I want to know more about this drone. What about battery life, control distance, speed and what about the FPV goggles sitting next to it?" Eyes now shifted to AJ who also had great knowledge of drones. "I also remember little things" he continued sarcastically.

Miles stared back knowing he was in for something pretty serious but he continued. "This drone will probably top out at twenty-five to thirty-five miles per hour. With the range extender, you can probably control this drone out to about 1,400 yards. It has an altitude holder, capable of returning to home if the pilot loses sight. Oh, there's something else to. This drone has what they call a follow-me, or active track system. This means that your device sends its location to the drone and as the object moves, the drone tracks and will follow you. The transmitter is pretty good as well, and it coordinates with the drone for the autonomous flying mode and automatic take-off and landing."

Nodding his head with a satisfied smile AJ then looked at his bro's and smiled. "How much weight will this drone carry?"

"Well, about seven or eight pounds I would say and that's pushing it and that it'll affect its flight distance, battery life, and altitude hold" Miles confided. In the silence, Miles wondered where the heck AJ learned so much about drones.

"What would it take to say light off a large firecracker or two from the transmitter if someone wanted to do that?"

"You mean dynamite?" Miles asked hesitantly.

"Whatever, just answer my damn question," he ordered impatiently.

"I dunno, I never tried to do anything like that before."

AJ then turned to a few of his boys, whispered something to them and left without any further words.

One of AJ's disciples with hands on his hips moved closer to Miles. "Well, little man, might as well get comfortable, because you ain't going anywhere for a while. Here's a pen and paper. Make a list of what you need to make this prototype so it'll fly," he said.

CHAPTER 23: Dragnet

As Omar was shuffling though yesterday's mail, he glanced down the hallway as Bernestine was twirling around to the beat of music from her head set. "Hey honey, good morning to ya," he whispered in a sexy tone while grinning. "Looks like someone is needing to go dancing!" he said, with his feet beginning to move towards his wife. "You know I still have a few steps left myself," he added, joining in the dance while following her lead.

Bernestine took of her headset as they both embraced, kissed and said good morning. "What ya holding there?" she inquired noticing Omar shuffling some letters in his hand. "Where did you find those? I told Kenny to get the mail yesterday and I never did see it."

"I found the mail in the family room on top of Kenny's play station as I was looking for the remote control. I don't even know why I keep trying to watch television there. Can't never find the remotes or they've done something so I can't get into my shows," he said while looking at the mail in his hands. "Have you seen Miles this morning? I want to talk to him about the letter he got from a place called Terrestrial Systems. Maybe it's a job?"

As Omar gave Bernestine her mail, Kenny came through with half-eaten toast hanging out of his mouth. Bernestine frowned. "How many times have I told you to eat the table? You're getting crumbs everywhere," she scolded, pointing to the closet where the vacuum was located.

"But Mom?" Kenny pleaded.

"But Kenny?" Omar repeated as he, too, pointed to the closet and smiled.

As Kenny pulled out the vacuum and began to run it, Bernestine called out to Miles, but there was no answer. "Kenny, have you seen Miles this morning? He's usually up by this time."

Kenny didn't hear a word as he was so single-minded and focused to get the vacuuming done so he could go and play.

"Kenny!" Bernestine said with a louder voice that got his attention.

Kenny turned off the vacuum.

"Have you seen Miles this morning?" she asked with a loud voice.

"No mom, not since yesterday when I saw him ride off on his bike. Said he was going over to Ralph's."

"I don't remember Miles asking to spend the night, but maybe he forgot?" Reaching for her cellphone, she called Miles but it went straight to his voice mail. "Hey honey will you please call Miles on the task force number? In the meantime, I'll check his room," Bernestine said while turning down the hallway. Climbing the stairs and entering Miles' room, she faintly smiled when she glanced in and making sure he just hadn't gotten up. With a deep sigh the aroma caught her nose off guard. "It's time to air out this room," she said, sniffing and making a face while opening up a window. She looked out across the bridge to the roof. Looking down, she picked up a pile of clothes and placed them in his hamper. "That boy of mine," she sighed, almost forgetting what she had come up to his room for.

Looking down her eye caught the blinking light from his personal cell phone. She noticed the number blinking was from her. Upon picking up the phone, she noticed the task force phone also blinking on the floor. It, too was a recent call from Omar. Her mind then switched immediately from worry about him being absent-minded to one of a mother's instinct. She picked up the micro GPS device next to the dirty socks, staring intently.

Returning downstairs with the three devices Bernestine had a worried look on her face. "I'll call over to Ralph's house, because that's probably where he's at," she muttered while dialing his number. Finding that he hadn't been seen since yesterday she looked at Omar who was fidgeting with some papers.

"I'll call a team meeting and between everyone he'll show up or someone will know where he is honey" while giving Bernestine a hug and heading for the door.

"I'll continue to call around and will call you if something comes up."

Omar immediately called a meeting with Katie; Ralph and the team leads to discuss the situation. "I told you all that this shit was gonna get nasty and you all promised to follow protocol, but now I find Miles's telephone is at home, his toe 911 communicator is in his room, and no one has seen him." His voice rose in volume and agitation. "We've put out a BOLO, I mean be on the lookout, but we need to stake out all the known gang hangouts. Hopefully that'll turn up something. How about you Ralph, you're his best friend - have you seen or talked with him?"

"No sir, I haven't seen him since we were having fun teaching some kids how to fly the micro's the other day."

"How about you, Katie?"

"That's the same for me, Mr. Johnson haven't seen him since the other day. I was carrying batteries for Miles and he forgot them so I caught up to him and rode with him for a while. This guy in the club, ah, Larry Wakefield, came up and the three of us chatted for a couple of minutes but I left one way and they rode off the other direction. It wasn't the normal way he usually rode home. I just figured he went to hang out with Larry."

"Do you know where this kid Larry hangs out or lives?"

"No, I don't. I've only seen him at the club, and he hasn't been coming as often as he used to."

"Could you identify him from a picture?"

"Sure, I could."

"Ok let's all go over to the communications room and we'll look at some pictures," Omar bellowed as he walked with his head down fearing the worse.

It didn't take long to ID Larry Wakefield and it was decided to put out an all-points bulletin with orders not to arrest and detain but to keep eyes on him.

"Katie and Ralph, from now on you keep your task cell phones on you at all times. You also wear the toe 911 devices. Do you have both of those items on you now?"

"Yes, sir," was the combined response.

"You team leads are now to tag along wherever these kids go when they leave their homes and have communications 24x7. That means keep your cell phones on and fully charged. If you need to leave home for any reason you call your team leads" he instructed with emphasis.

Liz abruptly entered the room and called Omar over to her. She looked furious and was looking down at a piece of paper she was reading from. With the look on Omar's face it was obvious that something horrific had happened and both Katie and Ralph thought it was bad news about Miles.

"Ok meeting is over. I've got something I need to do. Team leads set up communications with Katie and Ralph."

"Mr. Johnson, Mr. Johnson, is Miles ok?" Katie asked, shaken.

"It's ok dear, this news hopefully is not about Miles. You all go now and we'll be in touch."

CHAPTER 24: Prototype

Back at the command center, many individuals were crowded around viewing live television coverage, and talking to witnesses. There was a lot of activity, with people coming and going. A somber middle-aged man with silver hair reported, with his deep voice filling the room. "According to authorities, gang activity has increased to record levels lately, and we're being told that every young man arrested is armed with some sort of weapon, whether it be a knife, a gun, a baseball bat or a pipe." Somebody switched off the volume as the commander strode in.

Sitting amongst his peers, Omar listened intently as the commander began his somber message. "Yesterday we learned that someone, or maybe multiple people, were involved with bombings. A witness said that a drone landed on the hood of a car and when it pulled over, an occupant attempted to remove the drone when it blew up, killing and injuring multiple people. That evening it was reported that another drone flew into a window at a known gang members house and blew up as well. We are now in full condition red for Operation Sky Hawk. If we don't get a handle on this, it'll be totally taken over by the FBI. Like I said earlier, this was gonna get out of control, and now it's happened. God help us all."

The commander asked for status updates, going around the room. Nobody had much actionable intelligence, it was obvious. He decided that the team would look for Larry Wakefield at the club and that Katie would be given a GPS tracker to carry around with her in case she ran into Larry. She would approach him as though nothing had happened and place a micro GPS tracker on his bike.

168

That would enable the command center to observe his comings and goings. They watched his house and especially his going into what was considered a gang house. Everyone thought that Miles might be held at that location, but to confront the house at this time would endanger him even though plans were being drawn up to breach it. Larry showed up at the clubhouse a few hours later and only picked up a mini drone.

Katie rode over to him and asked how he was doing and he replied he was ok, but he hadn't been around because of family stuff. She purposely dropped a few drone blades on the ground and when Larry reached down to pick them up for her she placed the micro GPS button under his seat. When he looked up, he thought Katie was flirting with him but he was immediately told not to go there.

Katie reported this brief conversation with Larry and that he felt not only rushed but he seemed very defensive when she asked about Miles. "He said he didn't know where Miles was, and that he wasn't his babysitter and to go by his house and ask his parents." With that he just pedaled away in a hurry. The stakeout at Larry's house revealed that he only infrequently visited there and that he never spent the night. It also revealed that he was spending a lot of time at the house thought to be holding Miles. Cars were seen coming and going all hours of the day and night. Something big was happening and everyone was bracing for an assault on the house when communications were intercepted.

Larry was on his cell phone attempting to tell someone it wasn't his fault that Miles was taking so long to build the prototype but all the ordered parts were being sent out at a vacant warehouse. He said that he'd ride over to see what needed to be done and that Miles would only be taken there after everyone was sure the prototype was ready to be rebuilt.

Larry took off towards the warehouse, not knowing he was under surveillance. Upon arrival, he was shocked to see the entire floor space almost completely filled with drones in various stages of being put together. It didn't take long for him to understand that he and Miles were in big trouble and could possibly be killed by these people if those plans become jeopardized. Quickly, he pedaled back over to the house that Miles was being kept captive.

Miles appeared to be having trouble affixing the arms responsible for holding the guns when Larry entered. "Hey man I don't know what your problem is but if I were you, I'd get that damn prototype built. These dudes aren't playing and they're gonna kill us both if you don't hurry. What difference does it make to get that one done? You won't have to fly it."

"You know and I know they're gonna do us in when this is all said and done anyway, don't you?"

"What do you mean?"

"Don't act stupid Larry. If you hadn't stuck your nose in this crap we'd both be flying at the club instead of making these drones for war. I can't believe you're that stupid. Last night AJ came here and he was threatening to kill everyone in the house. He said that he was gonna get even with those that stabbed one of his boys so he sent a drone and blew up their car and their house with his new drones. He said that the dudes from the Midwest want all their money for them drones right now and that they aren't gonna wait much longer too. Said that he'd be damned if he was gonna loose the business deal of using them drones to deliver drugs and that that other gang is getting in their way. Now do you see what I'm talking about?" Miles said with a slow but deliberate way.

Just then, the door opened up and an individual came bursting in with a gun in his hand. As he was attempting to get around Larry he pointed the gun at his head and said he wasn't gonna ask him to get the hell out of his way. Stepping aside, the dude looked as though he was going to pistol whip Larry. He glared at Miles then at the table and back at Miles. "Your time is running out and if you aren't done tonight we'll do what we have to do without you or this asshole," again pointing his pistol at Larry. "I'll be back in a few hours so give me a reason and I'll be dusting your asses off," he added, looking back over his shoulder while slamming the door behind him.

"Now do you see what I mean, Larry?" Miles asked, studying the drone and bars over window. "It's all over for us and there isn't a chance we're gonna get out of here alive."

"Well, one things for sure. I just saw between twenty-five to fifty drones being assembled over at that empty warehouse and they're almost done, too. Many more in various stages of being put together in another room. Snooping around I saw an open crate filled to the brim with guns and..." but before Larry could finish the door opened up and in walked AJ with the dark shades and an armed escort.

Looking over at the table, the drone then Miles, he looked around the room. "Well, little man, you done?"

Larry said he was just asking him how much more time was needed and he was told to shut his mouth and get out in which he sidestepped everyone and walked briskly out the door.

Miles turned the drone around and finish attaching the brace and tightened it up with his small tools. "Yeah it's all done. The transmitter button is right here. It'll trigger the device that pulls the trigger once. The recoil because of the bump stock will chamber the rest of the bullets in that sequence until the drum or clip is empty."

"Are you sure this thing will fly? If it doesn't I'm coming back and you and I will finish our conversation," he threatened while his assistants picked up the drone and left. Miles could hear the door being locked so he knew he wasn't going anywhere.

The next couple of days things around the city got quiet. Kids who were known to be hanging out on the street corners or in drug areas went silent. It felt ominous. Something was brewing.

Meanwhile, because Larry had proven himself to the gang, he was told to show up to a peer initiation. He reluctantly did so, and soon found himself joining in with six other gang members, who began to circle a new member named Darius. Probably only sixteen years old, Darius seemed too short and slender for what was about to happen. The boy tried to grin, thinking he might smile his way through what was happening. He had proven himself to be worthy by shooting at a passing car that had dared to raise its high-beams as AJ rolled by. Darius had heard stories about what it took to join a gang, but he wasn't sure. He was about to be educated.

All at once, all seven members moved in and Jamal, one of AJ's trusted lieutenants, took charge. He had a red, black and green bandanna on his bald head, and his heavily-starched Levis hung low on his hips. He wore half-laced black boots with thick soles, and he seemed to be balancing on his heels. His left hand was behind his back, cradling a small, silver pistol that he was ready to pull out if needed.

Jamal took a breath, stared at Darius, and yelled "Beat down!"

Within seconds they knocked the kid down to the ground, followed by repeated kicks to both sides of his body and up and down his legs and arms. They jumped on him and screamed epitaphs. They were hoping he would begin to scream. Screaming or yelling for help meant you weren't ready for this gang, and you would be lucky to leave the circle alive.

Jamal noticed that Larry wasn't getting in as he should and called him out, pushing Larry forward with one hand, while the other hand began to slide the pistol out. Larry felt like running away but knew what would happen if he did. He then started kicking the poor individual on the ground but only with enough force that they wouldn't turn on him. Each time he kicked he got closer to crying.

Finally, Jamal put down Darius with an expert drop-kick, and the attack ebbed. Darius stopped squirming and began to roll over, breathing deeply. His shirt was ripped and smudged with dirt and blood. Larry noted the blood running out of his nose, and his face was beginning to swell along with his eyes closing.

Darius was helped to his wobbly feet and held up by leaning on two others. He used the back of his hand to wipe some blood from his nose, and nonchalantly wiped his hand on his jeans. He smiled weakly.

"Welcome home, bro!" they chanted in unison. With a growing smile, Darius pushed his helpers away and stood upright by himself. His eyes were continuing to swell shut, and blood still oozed from his lips and nose. But he had survived, and he was in.

Jamal turned to Larry, and with adrenaline still flowing, punched Larry on the arm. "You're next, bro, right after the war." Larry let a smile spread across his face, for fear of his doubts giving him away.

Sirens blared in the distance, and it was obvious that someone had called the police, so everyone scattered into the night.

As Larry rode his bike into the darkness, tears wouldn't stop flowing. "What did I do?" he kept saying to himself. "I turned in my friend, to join this gang, and now I help beat up a new member. What will happen to me?"

CHAPTER 25: Escape

Jumping the curb in front of his house as he often did on his bike Larry brought his bike to a screeching halt. As he sat looking up into the starlit night his silhouette was lit up from the moons rays as his observer took notes from his vehicle parked some vehicles away. "No, no, no, this isn't right" you could barely hear the audible message. With that he turned his bike around and rode off down the street with his pursuer in the distance. With heavy thoughts, he didn't notice he was being followed but he turned around and saw a black, tricked-out Chevy Impala, with wide gangsta wheels bulging from the sidewalls. The Chevy was trailing him without its headlights.

Turning abruptly around, the vehicle's lights came on, and it turned right at the corner and kept going. The driver called the other vehicle informing them that he had been made and that vehicle then took up the trailing and kept eyes on Larry.

About ten minutes later, Larry arrived where Miles was being held, the gang's main crib, known as The Bunker. Larry slowed down and got off his bike as quietly as he could, snuck up to the windows and peered in to see what kind of activity was going on. Music was playing loud and there were only a couple of home boys sitting around playing an old computer game. Two other boys were sprawled out on the couch asleep.

There were empty beer bottles, and cans everywhere. Creeping along the side of the house and to the back door he turned the nob slowly and discovered the door was not locked. In his attempt to open the door it squeaked with each push and he had to stop and start multiple times until it was wide enough to slip in. Once inside he looked left, then right looking for the key to where Miles was being held captive. About to give up, he stared at the door and to his surprise, the key was still in the lock. Tip toeing across the squeaky floor, he grabbed the key and turned it ever so gently and crept along the wall. He could barely see Miles lying on his side away from him. Larry reached down and put his hand over Miles' mouth to silence him.

Miles jolted away, eyes wide open in fear. "Shh, be quiet, dammit! Keep still," Larry warned, while looking back over his shoulder. "Get up quick. We have to get out of here now," Larry hissed.

Still trying to wake up, Miles followed Larry over to the door and as they peeked out, they saw a thug in the bathroom, bent over the toilet, apparently throwing up violently. It was John-John, who was known to have stomach troubles.

Larry and Miles stepped out into the hall, but their shadows gave them away. John-John turned and saw them, but he couldn't talk as he was too busy trying to catch his breath while emptying his stomach.

"Run, Miles, run," Larry screamed. He was out of breath, and all he could do was point to the door.

Several home-boys came running into the hallway. Larry and Miles scurried toward the back door, but that brought the household toward them, guns at the ready. Miles snatched the door open and began stepping through when gunshots erupted.

"Run Miles," Larry pleaded with a muffled voice as he slid down the wall onto the floor. Blood trickled from his mouth.

Outside Miles quickly started running as fast as he could without looking back. He tripped over Larry's bike in the darkness, but knew enough to grab the handlebars and get it rolling, then he jumped aboard and started pedaling furiously. He could still hear gun shots and a car squealing its tires as he ducked down an alley he knew quite well. After a few turns he slowed up and caught his breath.

As he pedaled, he looked back and saw headlights square up on the road behind him. He immediately ducked down a side street again. In complete darkness, he hid behind a fence as the car crept along the side street in hopes of finding him. Stepping out on the sidewalk again he jumped on his bike and pedaled as fast as he could and soon saw lights reflecting off the trees and houses. "Oh God, they found me," he trembled as he pedaled even faster.

The car caught up to him and then the siren came on. Looking back, he confirmed it was the police and he slammed on his brakes, still looking back from whence he came. The officer got out of his car and approached Miles with his flashlight pointing on his face. Out of breath, he tried to tell the officer what had just happened but his words didn't make any sense. "Uh, back there, they're chasing me. They shot me, no they shot at me. I think they killed my friend. Help me, help me," he cried out.

As the officer turned around to where Miles was pointing they both saw the lights of a car as it turned around squealing its tires in retreat. "Wow, slow down son, now who are you? What's going on?" the confused officer began.

"My name is Miles Watson" he stuttered. "My dad is Omar Johnson - he works out of Rampau Station," he added, remembering not to disclose the task force's location.

The officer looked closer at Miles and said to have a seat in his car as they both got in. Getting confirmation that Miles was who he said he was he placed his bike in the trunk and said he would take him home. As the officer responded to his radio he verified it was Miles he was transporting to his home. Arriving there both Bernestine and Omar were waiting outside. Miles ran into the arms of his mother hugging her, and both crying. Omar talked to the officer and got the details as to what had happened. The officer needed to respond to a call, turned to leave and Omar thanked him for bringing his son home. While they were talking another officer showed up stating he was being assigned to watch the house and with that everyone went inside.

"They shot him dad they shot Larry and I think they killed him" Miles cried while in his mother's arms. "They were shooting at me too but I was able to get away on Larry's bike. They're planning on a war using drones. I heard them, dad I heard them say the truce is over. AJ from the BBBs was saying the Alley Hogs and the Hood Rats are joining up against him and his boys. It's war!"

But before Omar could try to give Miles some reassurance, his cell phone went off. "I have to take this call," he said calmly, turning to smile at Bernestine and Miles. Mostly, he just listened and agreed, and with the call finished, he returned to the kitchen.

Bernestine reached out to hold his hand. "Miles has gone off to bed. If anyone needs to talk to him, it will have to wait."

Omar agreed. "Sure, this can wait. If I'm not here, tell him we raided the house where Miles was being held captive. We arrested some big guy who was sick, but everyone else was gone. His friend Larry wasn't killed, but he was shot a couple of times and he's on his way to the hospital, expected to live. I'm sure they'll station an officer outside his room for protection."

CHAPTER 26: Battle Plans

Miles was brought into the command center to share what he had picked up after being held for a week against his will. He was able to ID some of the individuals coming and going from the house. He had listened in one day when they were talking about twenty to thirty drone pilots that were getting proficient, with more being trained and ready for any call. He mentioned that he heard some arguing about attacking another gang because of the death of one of their own, but that was thwarted because the time wasn't right. Now, with two gangs joining forces against AJ, that could have all changed.

Larry was recovering at the hospital, but he identified the location of the drones that were being assembled. Rumor had it that the fence had supplied the Alley Hogs, Hood Rats, and BBBs equally, with the goal being to let them kill each other off and then move in while they were weak.

He said that he personally saw about fifty to one hundred drones being assembled. Some of the pilots being tested had flown drones for weed delivery and surveillance for robberies and that was successful, so the market was wide open. Larry thought that an attack was imminent, but didn't have a specific date but did say the assembly of drones was almost completed. He also confided that he had overheard AJ tell his top dawgs that they were given the contract to be the mule for some unknown top drug lord because BBBs had the most trained pilots.

This had angered the other two gangs, and started the increased killings. Lastly, Larry said AJ was planning to attack not only to get even but to take over the mule business completely. AJ had ordered everyone to the warehouse and to get ready for war.

As the commander began reviewing the maps it was calculated that any drone war would have to be in an area that would offer enough airspace, so he began to look at aerial maps for areas that were somewhat isolated, away from the main public's eye, a place that pilots would have a good line of sight and FVP capabilities, and especially an area where drones could be reasonably hidden.

The big break came when a real estate mogul named "Honest" Andy Jones was readying to sell an entire ten-building business park. It encompassed approximately 500,000 square feet. It was strategically located just off a highway, close to the flood plain, with easy road access in and out. To map the property, Honest Andy chose to use aerial photography, recording multiple videos of the site from different angles. The goal was to be one of the first to showcase their property using creative aerial views.

Once the SD card was retrieved, to his astonishment Jones saw what appeared to be birds flying around. Jones was new to the area, having recently been discharged from the Army, but he liked his job. A big man, constantly wearing pin-striped suits with a diamond-studded tie clasp, Jones usually wore an easy smile, but today his shiny face was creased with a frown. They had already overspent their bird damage budget caused by pigeons roosting in the eaves, and he didn't want to have to call the pest company again. While blowing up the pictures, Jones was stunned to find out that they weren't birds after all. They were drones.

Jones had decided to take a drive over to the property and check it out. As he drove his Cadillac into the complex, he noticed some people across the site that looked like workers. Parking his car, he walked alongside two of his buildings. He soon noticed activity coming and going out of one of the loading dock bays. Moving closer but keeping a low profile, difficult for a man of his girth, he then noticed drones coming out of bay number nineteen a couple of drones flew into bay thirty-three. "What the hell?" he said to himself as he backed out slowly and returned to his car. "Those look like guns hanging from the drones." He immediately returned to his office, scooped up the SD card and his maps and photos, and squealed to a stop in front of the nearest police station.

Omar happened to be leaving the commanders office when he was called over to the desk sergeant. "Hey Omar, you got to listen to what this gentleman has to say," the sergeant said.

Looking at the realtor, and the desk sergeant, Omar invited him into the commander's office. They closed the door and dimmed the lights to view the video. At the end of the presentation, the commander looked at the realtor. "Do you know how long these drones have been flying around your property?"

Jones shook his head. "No, but the site has been empty for about a year-and-a-half. We haven't been able to sell the property and thought we'd fly the area again to create some excitement," he continued. "We decided if we couldn't sell this parcel we'd tear it down and make way for a mall. Guess we'll have to increase our security team. They only drive that area about once a week, if that, but we can rearrange that schedule and if that activity is happening we'll get it stopped," he said irritably.

The commander started to think about all of this and then said, "How about we have our officers check on your property on a regular basis? That should save you on paying for these services. This property is within our jurisdiction, but what we'll need from you are these pictures, video and to keep this confidential. What ya think?"

Jones liked the idea of saving money. "I'll give my boss a call, but he'll be fine," the big man said.

Agreement in place, they thanked the realtor for coming in and then began studying the photos again. "Call an entire team meeting for tomorrow before we lose complete control of this mess," the commander ordered.

As Omar addressed his team, minus Miles, Katie and Ralph, he walked over to the blown-up map. "We now have evidence that the gangs are using vacant warehouses for illicit activity. Don't know how long, but it has been confirmed through these pictures. We also have some unconfirmed reports that drugs have been arriving and being stored in one of the ten vacant buildings. We're guessing that sooner or later drones will be used for deliveries."

Omar shook his head in disbelief. "We've intercepted some intel that there are three groups -- the BBBs, and two smaller gangs, the Alley Hogs, and the Hood Rats. The two smaller gangs seem to have joined forces against the BBBs. We haven't been able to obtain their names or call signs. They are all vying for territorial control, and they may be gearing up for a final war. We do know that one of the gangs is using this site for their base operations, but we haven't located the other two groups yet."

Studying the map once again, he looked over at his commander. "As of today, we're assigning all available units to Operation Sky Hawk," he said while pointing to the target quadrant. "As of tonight, we're going to have someone perched at the water tower as our eyes and ears. The workers already encased the lower portion with a construction curtain while they work on it, so we're going to take it over. We'll have a 360-degree view and the half dome on top has an inner shell that will protect anyone from the elements as well as hide them from the ground. There's a walkway surrounding the exterior but we won't be using that until we absolutely need to. There shouldn't be any traffic coming and going as that place has been closed for years. I want every vehicle photographed and documented so we know how long they stay in this compound and where they go once they're in it. According to this recent photo, there are only four ways in and out so that goes for this effort as well. Ok, team assignments are on the wall. Good luck, stay in communication and take no unauthorized risks." Omar dismissed the group.

As Operation Sky Hawk got under way, plans were being put together based upon the intel being received daily. From the water tower reports, activity was increasing especially in and out of building seven that had thirty bays. The observer couldn't tell if it was the same drone or multiple drones that were flying at low level. Also, buildings outside the grid they called them building A and B, had vans pulling in and unloading crates. The exterior of the vans had the markings of Kennedy Plumbing. The other had the name of Ben's concrete cutting. They both appeared to be legitimate work crews so not much attention other than photographing the vans and documenting their time in and out. Lastly three very large dumpsters were dropped off at these sites. They were the ones that the sides dropped down versus open top dumpsters. It appears they're going to forklift something in or out of them. This continued increase of activity brought the full-scale alert to Operation Sky Hawk.

The briefing room was now filled completely, with some attendees standing at the back. There was the gang task force, the tactical SWAT team, fire and rescue, and even the mayor, who had taken a keen interest.

To gain full aerial advantage, Omar announced that the water tower would be used as the launch site when the incursion started. Because of the half-moon top and 360-degree walkway, it would be a perfect vantage point for aerial defense.

At that moment, Liz walked in. Omar hadn't seen her for several days, he realized. She was dressed in ninja black, and she took off her black watch cap and began talking and pointing to spots on the map. "I visited the area just now and did some recon. Building two has a large breeze way capable of flying multiple drones out of the loading bay. Building seven, with its thirty door loading berths, would be perfect for a massive assault. Building A has the three-large side open dumpsters with heavy increased activity. Building B has a three-sided blind area, but is open to the sky."

"How did you get all that information?" the mayor asked.

"I spent the last three nights roaming all ten buildings inside the grid. I also used my infra-red and thermal imaging equipment on everything encountered. I counted at least 100 drones, most of which appear ready to fly armed. There were others that instead of cameras hanging from their bottoms look like they had neatly packed containers, probably explosives, or at least that's what I think they were. What I don't understand is that building A, near the three large dumpsters, has a couple of school busses that came and went. They stopped there as well as at building B. Then some twenty or so people went on to the roof. My guess is that they were realtors on a show me trip," he guessed.

"Liz, please have your team check with the realtors to halt their access," Omar instructed. "We don't want them blundering into a disaster."

Looking at the map, he paused and took a breath. "Because of the activity outside of the grid, we'll need to keep our eye to the east and west highway to the north. The road northwest and south will have to be shut down, and also behind the water tower the east and west side streets will have to be covered at a moment's notice. Make sure that treed area and that swamp have eyes on them, and watch for somebody out walking their dog or out jogging the trails. We will place our SWAT teams on the water tower, building eight, and buildings C and D, since those are the tallest structures. Any questions?" Omar inquired.

Liz looked concerned. "If these gang members are gearing up for a drone war, and if they launch an attack on each other, there is no way we have the resources to engage them all, because we don't have enough trained drone pilots. We sure as hell can't shoot them down with side arms and long guns," she added.

Omar nodded. "This is war!" he barked. "At all costs, we have to keep them contained in this grid, even if we need to use water cannons to shoot them out of the sky," he thundered.

Liz walked over to the map and frowned. She felt overwhelmed.

A uniformed officer slipped into the room ahead of a young black man dressed in camouflage gear. The officer handed Omar a note, then left the room, leaving the young man standing awkwardly, carrying a heavy satchel.

Omar read to himself, then addressed the room. "We've just learned that besides our own aerial drone defense team, we've obtained a new defensive weapon. I'd like you to meet specialist Javari Barnes from Homeland Security." The room fell silent.

Barnes removed his hat, revealing a boyish, athletic face. He pulled his satchel to the table and began unpacking what looked like a space-age sniper rifle. "This device is called an ADK – an anti-drone killer," he began. "It looks like a rifle, but you can see it has what looks like a hedge clipper at the end of the barrel. These are actually antennas," he said.

Then he pointed to the underside of the gun, which looked like a large, black box. "This underbelly contains a computer with a de-scrambling program. You simply aim, lock on through the screen here," he said, pointing, "and when you pull the trigger, a destructive, non-kinetic energy beam shoots out. It will knock a drone out of the sky from 300 meters by homing in on its transmitter frequency and frying the electronics."

Omar and several other veterans shook their heads in marvel. The younger occupants in the room took the ADK in stride – it made perfect sense.

"We only have two of these weapons, but they should even up the odds quite a bit," Barnes added.

CHAPTER 27: War

Listening devices placed at strategic locations revealed that there was a surge in activity at ground zero. People were scattering everywhere and the buses had been parked now for a couple of days behind building A and B. This was confirmed by the water tower observer. Eight vans had also shown up to the bays of building seven. It was now evident that they were getting ready to square off.

Omar decided to pre-position everyone because it now seemed obvious that an assault was being planned for the upcoming weekend, regardless of what gang started the attack. With this news, Omar approached his commander. "If these gangs launch all them drones at once, there is no way our small team will be able to take on that many drones. A massive assault on the pilots might work, but they can launch from one to two miles away so that's not gonna happen. We need to get them all within our sphere of control. I'd like to share with you a plan that I've been working on. It's going to include the three kids and I think it might work."

But before Omar could continue he was abruptly interrupted. "Oh, hell no! Are you crazy? We can't expose those kids to this mess, there's gonna be a lot of gunfire and you even want to expose your son Miles? What the hell kind of dad are you?" the commander scolded.

"Come on, at least hear me out, commander. These kids are some of the best pilots we have. They're our best chance."

"So, you're wanting to let them fire live ammunition and possibly kill others?"

Agitated, Omar slapped the desk. "No dammit! They'll be flying the drones with radio disrupters, no guns. That's what we've been training for."

"How you going to keep them out of harm's way?"

"Come over here and take a look at this plan. I'm thinking of placing Miles, Katie, and Ralph inside the water tower. That's where we've been stockpiling our drones. They'll be wearing those new first-person view goggles, and will be high enough if they need to go out to fly by line of sight. Their team leads will fly from their perches and will be followed by the kids in case they get overpowered. So, we'll have three aerial observers who will fly their quads at high altitude and communicate down to the team leads and kids. They will also be videotaping the action. We'll have nine gunship drones each carrying a fifty-round drum. We've calculated that once this mess starts each drone will only have approximately ten minutes of actual air time and each one of our team will be assigned two drones. That'll give us the ability to stay in the fray. We will have enough ground forces to prevent anyone from leaving this quadrant as well. We'll put those two new ADKs on the rifle platform. And finally, we'll have enough snipers perched with full view to take out any threats, drones or individuals. So, what ya think?"

The commander studying the map that Omar had brought just shook his head. "God help us if this is our future. When you going to tell the kids they're in?"

"I've already told them, and they're in transit as we speak," Omar confessed.

The commander just stared. "Kids flying drones. ADKs. Snipers. Any more, new gadgets?"

Omar grinned. "Did I mention the phased plasma rifles in da 40-watt range?" he smiled, mimicking an old Arnold Schwarzenegger movie.

"Omar, if you fail, don't come back," the commander said with a partial grin and consent.

Omar returned to the base of operations, had Katie, Miles and Ralph called and prepared for the inevitable. "Ok, Operation Sky Hawk is under way. You've seen the presentations so you know how serious this is gonna get. We or rather I do not want to put you in harm's way, so if you're in, you must promise to follow instructions given to you by your team leads, myself or anyone else in authority. Is that perfectly clear?" he asked with a stern voice.

After hearing "Yes!" from all three kids, he revealed the final plans. "Looks like we're gonna possibly be up against fifty to one hundred or more drones. All of these will be armed, some with explosives, many with guns. Because of this I want you elevated high enough to be out of the direct action. We've updated your new goggles with stronger communication abilities, as well as increased florescence so you'll be able to see sharper images if you go by line of sight. As we've practiced before, you'll all be assigned special radio frequencies. One more note. Once you receive your transmitter, remove the two protective caps. Remember only push the red button if you lose sight of your drone or it malfunctions and falls out of the sky. The satellite will do the rest. Tap once for the drone and don't tap twice or your transmitter will fry as well."

Miles, Katie and Ralph all nodded silently.

"Oh, one more trick we'll have at our disposal. There will be three extra drones pre-positioned, armed and ready to be flown in a situation that we become overwhelmed and we're out of power. Each transmitter will have an emergency black switch and once activated it'll automatically fly to the last known position of the transmitter's message and be ready for engagement. Everyone has practiced this maneuver, however if it's one of you kids that launches the drone it will know from which transmitter it came from and will auto disengage live fire and switch to frequency disrupter. As I mentioned before, you kids will not be allowed to do live firing, to take someone's life, period, no discussion."

There was silence. He remembered the newest gadget. "Hey, one more asset we just got from Homeland Security. They have a new ADK – Anti-Drone Killer."

"Say what?" Katie asked.

"ADK. It's new technology that can lock onto a drone's transmission signal and fry the electronics. We haven't had a chance to train with them, so they'll be off your frequency and only in contact with the command center."

Taking a few minutes for the trio to absorb this information, Omar looked out at the kids and map. "Its gonna get messy out there and this is why we've made a few changes to the original plans. They've been doing some maintenance work so the water tower's base is encased entirely so no one will be able to see behind the opaque screens. I hope you're not afraid of heights," he continued with a you-asked-for-it grin.

"Don't worry, there's a temporary elevator so you won't have to climb the ladder. Ralph, there's room up there for your chair as well. You'll be flying from the open nodule so you'll have full view of this area. All of you will still have your team leads who will fly from buildings five, six, and eight. Your team lead will get communication from the high-flying aerialists who will relay coordinates. They are the same ones you've trained with during the training out in the valley. Each team will have three gunships, and you with your radio frequency disruptors. Remember when your special alarm goes off, immediately hit the Return-to-home button and your drones will fly back to the catch net below the tower. If you lose sight and can't recall your drone, immediately push this button on your transmitter. Then launch your second drone and get back into the action. Just like you've been practicing, follow your team lead and keep them safe. Oh! One more piece of instruction. No free styling until your given the go-ahead from your team lead."

Omar turned back to view the map and look at the overwhelmed faces of Miles, Katie and Ralph. "I'll be in the van that will be used as our onsite communication's vehicle and I'll be seeing everything on screen so good luck everyone. Stay safe" while staring at Miles specifically.

At exactly 1530 hours, sensors picked up activity followed by an intercepted call saying that war had just been declared and it would be coming from the air. That triggered a call to the command center and to the water tower to validate if there was any increased activity. The sides of two semi-trailers plopped open and two large-scale dumpsters likewise dropped their sides. Soon countless drones were airborne with no coordinated movements. At first count, Omar estimated that twenty to twenty-five drones were all circling and moving toward the center of the business park.

They were met by as many drones from building seven and five which began to form a wobbly line of defense. Within minutes gunfire erupted, some single shots and only a few rapid fired as they hadn't had time to arm everyone. Drone war commenced and the sky was filled with at least one hundred drones engaged in aerial combat. It was obvious from the command centers high aerial observers that the gang pilots were not very experienced and oftentimes they shot in the blind in hopes of striking something. Every once in a while, you could hear the ping of bullets striking a drone and see it crash into the ground or a building but it was luck more than skill. Some very inexperienced pilots flew their drones into the high-power lines because they were flying by line of sight and lost track of their path. Others crashed into each other not knowing how to get out of the way.

"Are you ready kids?" a call came in from one of the aerial flyers. "Hook up with your team leads." Katie, Ralph and Miles took off from the water tower and dropped down to meet up with their team leads. Hanging just a few yards back, Katie's lead Kendra caught up to a drone and with a blast sent it crashing to the ground.

"Ok, here we go. Katie, drop in behind me off to my right," Kendra commanded with an elevated voice.

"I'm already there," was the anxious reply.

Kendra turned slightly to the left, and with a quick burst sent a drone crashing to the ground. With a quick 360-degree turn there were three drones just hovering nearby as if not knowing what to do and she dispatched them swiftly. A drone attempted to crash into her but missed. "You see that drone attempting to turn back on me, Katie?"

"I see it, I see it."

"It's right under you. Drop down and take it out, I'll maneuver out of the way and if you miss it, I got it."

In her excitement, Katie dropped too low and temporarily lost sight of her intended target. She quickly regained altitude. Heart pounding and her controller shaking, Katie took a deep breath, caught up to the rogue drone, locked on it and fired. To her surprise it shook once then dove into the ground with pieces flying everywhere. "I did it, I did it," she hollered enthusiastically.

"Good job, Katie," Kendra said. "Now follow me, we're being sent across the parking lot."

Grady received an urgent call from his aerial observer stating that about ten drones were buzzing in and out of the trees and getting close to the water tower. "Miles, you see those drones slipping in and out of the trees along the gully?"

"No, not yet," Miles replied, while turning his drone around. They soon appeared on his screen, hovering with menace. "Ok, I see them," he said with a cracked voice.

"Ok, here's what I want you to do. Split off from me. I'll chase them from the trees and if they dodge beneath the bridge, you'll have them in plain sight if they emerge. Remove your safety switch so you're ready to engage. Split off now," Grady commanded.

Immediately, Miles headed to the other side of the bridge and held his ground. Just as Grady had predicted, four drones appeared in formation. They hadn't noticed him at first so he dropped down, locked on and took two out of action. The third attempted to shoot him down, but missed. Before he could turn to reengage, two drones just dropped out of the sky.

"What just happened?" Miles asked. "They just dropped."

Grady broke in. "That was the ADK stationed along-side the bridge that took them out. I've got trouble here!" he shouted.

Grady was being over whelmed with numbers, dodging gunfire and suicide drones frantically. Miles flew through four or five drones, meandering as if lost and trying to get into the fray.

Hovering for a brief moment, he aimed and took them out one by one, as if playing a video game.

The aerial observer reacted with a chuckle. "Way to go Miles," the mechanical voice said. That brought a genuine smile on Omar's face while he was monitoring the situation.

As Grady and Miles caught up to each other, Grady scanned the skies. "Miles, there's just too many of them for us to fly tandem. Just a minute, hold your altitude. I'll check in with our observer."

"Way too many," Miles agreed. He hovered in place, checking on his battery. He had a half charge remaining.

The mechanical voice of the aerial observer returned. "It looks like the odds are about seven to one," he said calmly. "Grady, you are free to go solo in your sector. Good hunting. Out."

"Got that Miles? Go for it," Grady said excitedly.

Miles began to hum *Pushing Mach 5* as he did a 360 turn and the battle appeared to have slowed down to a frame. Immediately he began to take down drones, one, two, three, then four, five and six drones. His transmitter began to beep alerting him his battery was draining and he pushed a button and his drone returned to the catch net below. It didn't take long for him to launch his second drone, seeking out new targets.

Arlan and Ralph had their hands full when Ralph saw three drones pull out of the fight and head into a loading bay in building number two. He broke off, chasing them while Arlan was engaged and taking out drones that were shooting wildly. "Ralph, where are you?" he muttered while scanning the skies.

"I'm off to your right about to chase three drones into a building. They have some sort of box underneath them," Ralph said happily.

"What? Stop, NOW! Pull back immediately" came the garbled order.

Ralph continued to chase and was closing in on them, but he wasn't close enough yet to lock on. Just a few more yards he figured, as he flipped the safety switch on his transmitter. It began to vibrate when a screech then a loud voice rang into his headset. "STOP! STOP!" yelled Arlan. "Pull back now," he demanded.

Confused, Ralph removed his finger, hovered and backed up quickly. Within seconds two suicide drones detonated their explosives inside building number two. Ralph's drone wobbled due to the blast wave.

Shaken, Ralph turned his drone around and zoomed in on Arlan's drone. "Wow, that was close," he said weakly.

"You ok?"

"Yeah, I'm good."

"Ok, then let's go," Arlan replied after being dispatched across to the other quadrant to another hot spot.

As if things couldn't get any worse, the command center interrupted all conversation with an urgent order that came blasting into everyone's headsets. "More drones have just been launched and they're carrying explosives! You are to seek them out and destroy them."

An aerial observer surveying his sector noticed what appeared to be drones hovering just above the ground, close to Katie and Kendra. "Katie, off to your left about ten feet off the ground two drones are hovering and creeping along the ravine."

"I see them," she said calmly, as one began to climb and hover above a police van as if trying to figure out how to lower itself for detonation. As it began to lose altitude it began to wobble, a sure sign of an inexperienced pilot. Katie swooped down, locking on target. "I got you now," she said, pushing off the safety toggle on the transmitter. She let fly, and adjusting her camera, she saw the powerless drone fall to the ground without exploding. She was jolted when her alarm went off, notifying her that the power was drained and the drone was returning home. Within a minute she was airborne again, combing the battle grid for action.

A pilot from the BBB's just happened to be looking eastward towards the water tower when he thought he saw birds coming and going from its opening. Looking closer, he realized they were drones, so he quickly diverted his drone and called for another flyer to follow upward from the trees behind building B.

As the pair rose closer, they were observed by Jason, another of the aerial observers. Jason was about to dispatch Grady, but sensing that he was actually the closest, and that time was of the essence. Jason readied his aim at the closest drone, locked on it and pushed the button, but nothing happened.

Again, he pushed the button, but again there was no response. Taking a deep breath, he watched as the enemy drone climbed almost to the tower's opening. With full throttle, Jason plowed his drone into the enemy and both crashed some eighty feet to the ground. "I'm out of action," he hollered over the headsets. "There's another drone here that discovered the water tower. Someone get over here quickly," he demanded.

Miles quickly arrived and pointed his camera upward. "I see it, and I got it," he mumbled. With his customary humming, he punched the throttle and rose to meet his challenger. The other drone seemed to sense him coming in, and turned to face him, but Miles was already locked on. With the push of a button, the disrupter engaged and Miles sent the drone tumbling to the ground.

The shooting and whining of drone motors began to die down, and as Omar viewed the monitors inside the command center van, he began to realize that even with the overwhelming odds, his team owned the skies. Drones were dropping out of the sky continually, raining down. Others were flying with uncertain moves, indicating to Omar that they were flown by inexperienced pilots. Apparently, the gang pilots hadn't practiced using specific radio frequencies and coordination. Without their overwhelming numbers, they were much less effective. Now, when a pilot made a move, multiple drones inadvertently did the same move. Most oftentimes they became sitting ducks.

Omar commanded the ground forces to start moving in, and they soon completely surrounded buildings A and B. Buildings two and seven attempted to launch a couple more drones from the open bay, but were taken down immediately by a member from the ADK team. The few other drones that were able to get airborne posed no threat because they had no armaments and were apparently sent out as decoys.

Jason had seen it all and alerted the ground forces. When the order came to breach, all three gangs launch sites were assaulted at the same time. It was quick and surgical. All in all, some seventy culprits were rounded up, cuffed and processed for transporting to jail.

All of a sudden two drones appeared out of nowhere, both carrying bump stock technology. They were observed by the fire department crew, which had done little so far. Using high-pressure water cannons, the firemen knocked the two drones down, and shared some hearty high-fives.

As soon as the remaining aerial observers cleared the air, they gave the all clear signal to the command center and team members began showing themselves from their perches. As Omar looked at the monitors for the last time and took off his head set. He let out a giant exhale and exited the command center.

Stepping out in the fresh air, the sun was just setting and he took a deep breath, somewhat anxious but relieved it was over. Looking first toward the water tower then surveying the rooftops, a silent sense of relief came over him. As he began to walk across the yard towards the water tower a familiar sound caught his attention. An observation drone circled above him lazily; he guessed it was Jason.

Then with a snarling buzz, three more drones appeared out of nowhere in front of hm. Quickly realizing they weren't his, he asked for backup, but realized he was no longer wearing his headset. Two drones were carrying guns with bump stocks, and the third had a gun and an explosive charge attached to its underbelly. "Ah, shit," he muttered, attempting to find a hiding place.

The three drones locked onto Omar and began to shoot wildly but without success. Dirt flew near his feet and bark chipped away from the nearby trees. Jason saw the action on his screen and sat up in his seat. The observer drone jolted into action and dove into the suicide drone, which exploded noisily.

The fireball caught the attention of Katie. She had been circling around in long loops, but she now eagerly joined in the fray. Omar was being pinned down by one of the drones using single fire, while the other drone was closing in.

Miles saw in horror what was happening, but he had used up his two drones. He looked on helplessly. Running along the catwalk he called out. "Dad, dad, look out! Take cover in the trees," he screamed.

Katie's drone dove down and locked on the rogue that was shooting single shots at Omar. She powered in on a long dive and quickly knocked it out of the sky. But that was the last of her battery, and she was forced to return to the netting. She called out to her lead in alarm. "Base, base, we need help in the trees by the tower. The boss is pinned down in the trees!"

The remaining drone now had a clear shot at Omar and spat out short bursts that flushed him from behind a tree. He dodged and ran left, but the drone followed with another short burst. When he stopped, it too stopped, hovering some thirty feet above him. He frantically looked for better cover, then darted as fast as he could into a cluster of bigger trees. Bullets sprayed into the wood that protected him.

Seeing the water tower high above the trees he mumbled to himself. "If I sprint from the trees to the safety net, I'll be safe," he decided. He began to run down the trail, sticking close to the trees for cover. Feeling he had lost the attacking drone, he started walking while looking over his shoulders.

"Dad, dad, stay in the trees," Miles hollered, looking down and hanging on to the railing. Omar could hear him as he began to step out in an opening. Seeing a shadow of the drone on the ground, he ducked back into the trees looking left, then right. He again started running down the path, hoping the drone wouldn't follow him, but it was right on his back. He dove behind a tree just as the drone sent another small hail of bullets into the trunk.

Panting, he peeked his head around the tree trunk and there was the drone, seeking him out. With his back against the trunk he saw a tight opening, so he quickly pushed some bushes out of the way and ducked and weaved deeper into the darkness. What he hadn't realized was that the drone didn't need to meander underneath the bushes as it just elevated above him and waited for the right moment.

Kendra had been alerted from her position and could see everyone pointing to the bank of trees. Thanks to her previous combat experience, she calmly assessed the situation. "If I were Omar, I'd lead that rogue away from the kids," she thought aloud. "I'd run to that small cluster of trees with that tight canopy," she added, while throttling up her drone.

As she moved to a spot near the cluster of trees, her battery alarm went off. Omar made a dash for the canopy and as the enemy drone began to lower itself, she was right there. She flipped an override switch to prevent her drone from automatically retreating, knowing that would give her just one chance at her target. She hovered patiently, and spotted the enemy coming into range. She held her breath, locked on, and pushed the button on her transmitter.

Nothing happened. Instead of a kill shot, she watched helplessly as her drone dropped out of the sky.

Katie began yelling at Miles as she came from the back of the water tower walkway. "Launch the pre-positioned drone quickly," she said, pointing down.

Disoriented and confused, Miles just stood there, looking down at the ground and thinking his dad was dead. His transmitter banged against the railing, which brought him back to his senses. Frantically, he looked into Katie's eyes and he read her lips. "Launch the pre-positioned drone NOW."

Miles looked down at his transmitter and pushed the appropriate button but nothing happened. He desperately pushed it again, complaining that it wasn't working. "My dad, my dad," he hollered. "Where's the drone, I don't see it!" he shouted.

"Over there, right there" Katie pointed urgently. "Hurry up."

"I see it. I got it. OK, I got it." He moved steadily now. Miles flashed back to the captors, the house where AJ had told him it was he who had flown drones to explode a car and into a house. He then realized the pilot chasing his dad was AJ, because he knew all the tricks. As he clenched his teeth he frowned, then readjusted his goggles. "I told you I'd get you," he hollered into his headset. "I told you."

AJ sensed the intruder and turned his drone around to confront his pursuer. He let off a short burst which missed, then turned back to his business with Omar. AJ saw his target start running again, and he took chase. Flying close quarters around trees, through branches, going high, then low, hugging the ground, nothing deterred AJ from closing in on Omar. As he got in range, he readied his drone a kill shot, but Omar ducked back into a tight cluster of trees and started sprinting down the trail, dodging and weaving, with the drone attempting to lock on.

Omar dove into a dark area and curled up tightly. AJ lost sight of him, but saw that the nimble drone was still chasing him. Knowing he couldn't get Omar while being chased by this new drone, AJ decided to attempt to shake it with maneuvers only a talented pilot would pull off. He buzzed through branches and around rocks, only to see that the pesky drone was right on him.

AJ assumed that it had to be Miles at the controls. "You're good, but not that good!" AJ said as he climbed, then dove straight to the ground and halted, hovering only a few feet in the air behind a stump. Miles shot by, momentarily losing him.

"I told you I'm the better pilot," AJ said, turning back to Omar, who he now saw was peering around a tree. Locking on his target he was confident he had him this time. He steadily moved in for the kill. He sprayed the area with a long burst, but the gun stopped shooting before his finger came off the trigger, so he knew he was out of bullets. But he still had his explosive charge.

He moved his thumb to the button and eased toward Omar, who was peering out from the tree again. Omar could hear the hum of the drone's motors as it drew closer. AJ figured he'd have to get right on top of Omar for the blast to be effective, and with a confident and arrogant smirk, he prepared to push the detonation button. He just needed another ten yards, he figured.

Miles swooped back behind AJ and got him in his sights. The enemy drone filled his screen when he sent out the kill shot.

Omar ducked back behind the tree trunk and curled into a ball, hands clutching his head.

AJ cursed as his drone tumbled to the ground, far short of its target. He managed to get the detonation signal to the drone, and it hit the ground with huge explosion.

Miles' transmitter flashed, alerting him his battery was discharged and all he could do was perform a 360 view in hopes of seeing his dad. But the only thing he saw was a cloud of dust created by the blast. Then the screen went blank as his drone dropped out of the sky. Dropping his transmitter on the walkway, he and Katie both had tears in their eyes, as they embraced. Miles was sobbing and cursing at the same time.

"Hey, you up there. Is anyone left?" Omar yelled, while brushing off his clothes and wiping his glasses.

Katie and Miles quickly broke free from each other, sheepishly staring deeply into each other's eyes.

Miles quickly regained his composure and looked down at Omar. "I was afraid you were a goner," he called down.

"Well, my ears are ringing, that's for sure," Omar said calmly.

Katie laughed. "Good thing there are some war pilots covering your old ass from the sky," she called out.

Miles chuckled with a big grin. His gaze fell to Katie's T-shirt and he smiled even wider. It read CLEARED FOR TOUCH AND GO.

Omar looked upwards waved both arms in relief. "I'm too old for all of this," he declared. He bent down to tie a shoe.

All of a sudden, two shots rang out, spitting up dirt behind him. If he hadn't ducked down, he would have been hit. Spinning around, the only safe spot was back in the trees, so he darted back for cover. "Take cover, you two," he called out from the trees.

"Run dad, run," Miles hollered while desperately looking for help. But all the drones now were out of service and the ADK's were all off line as well.

Omar knew he was once again being hunted as he tiptoed amongst the trees. But there were no drones in the skies that his ears could detect. He stayed extra quiet and kept to the shadows, still worried about the kids on the tower.

More single shots rang out below them, and each crack was like a whip to Miles and Katie. They huddled against the water tower, behind the cover. Where were the shots coming from?

AJ had exhausted the bullets from his pistol and pulled out his knife in rage. As he scanned his surroundings, he saw one of his drones with an AR-5 strapped to it with a bump stock. With the strength of a mad man he yanked it free and continued to pursue Omar. Moving stealthily, he barely saw Omar's silhouette as he moved between some trees. "You son-of-a-bitch," he said under his breath. "You've messed with me for the last time, old man!"

Omar dove into a dark thicket and curled himself into a tight ball. He had no idea if he was visible or not. "How's your day going, AJ?" he yelled out.

AJ was furious. "A lot better than yours, grampa!" he spat out. He sighted Omar's form. He raised his weapon, steadied for a shot, and then fired. A burst of rapid gunfire echoed throughout the trees.

"You missed, AJ!" Omar cried out. He dove to the ground next to a rotten log just as another hail of bullets ricocheted off the bark. Moving lower for better cover, Omar stuck his head out to see where the shots were coming from. As he did he looked right into the eyes of AJ who was pointing the gun directly at him.

"Got you now!" AJ crowed triumphantly. His finger was poised on the trigger.

Crack! One single shot rang out. Omar flinched, expecting pain, and bumped his head against the log. He opened his eyes and saw AJ's head look up into the night sky, then fall backwards, eyes open, as he fell to the ground next to his weapon.

SWAT team members burst onto the scene with laser dots lit up on Omar's body. With both hands up in the air he hollered. "It's me Omar. It's me," he said, this time with an exhausted voice. Slowly, the squad members lowered their weapons, while one bent down to ensure AJ was lifeless and kick aside the gun.

Omar was escorted to the clearing beneath the water tower, into a barrage of flood lights that had been turned on. For the first time, high above the ground, Miles, Katie, Ralph realized Omar was safe. They hollered down, waving with joy.

Omar looked up as best he could through the bright lights and gave a wave and nod back to them for a job well done.

As the trio took the service elevator down, they were able to survey the battlefield, see the smoke from the smoldering buildings, and saw law enforcement officials meandering everywhere. They were met by Omar and they all hugged with the warmest embrace.

"Everyone ok?" he inquired.

"We are now" the trio said simultaneously, as Ralph performed enthusiastic 360's.

CHAPTER 27: Aftermath

The next morning, the newspapers and television newscasters were all reporting on the all-out gang war, with many casualties, property damage and the biggest drug raid in quite some time. That evening the entire Operation Skyhawk team was called to the command center. Miles, Katie and Ralph were ordered to report to the small glassed-in room near the back where they could observe without being seen.

Soon all the parents were ushered in and were greeted by their kids. Bernestine was beaming; Kenny was also there, and it was clear he was very proud of his big brother.

Liz appeared as well, but this time there was no business look on her face. Instead, she was very gracious and smiled, looking deeply into each of the kids' eyes. "We could not have gotten through this ordeal without you three kick-ass pilots," she declared, then grew somewhat embarrassed for cussing.

She looked at the parents. "Thank you so much for your dedication. There will be more, but I wanted to say this before the program starts. Unfortunately, you'll have to observe from here as stated earlier, because we want you to remain anonymous."

As Mayor Hansen was introduced, he walked to the front the room. He was an older and taller version of Omar, slightly overweight, with shades of white hair at the temples that framed an eternal smile. As he prepared to address the dignitaries, he took a few seconds to briefly look at the back of the room. "This city owes a great gratitude to each and every one of you for a job well done. You've all participated and witnessed a new source of fear and horror. Turning recreational drones into weapons. My God what's the world coming to? We must ensure that this technology doesn't become a regular occurrence. What a nightmare" he yelled with emphasis. Taking a sip of water, he stared out at the crowd and continued. "From what I've been told, this was the biggest drug haul this city has ever seen."

As the Mayor looked over his shoulder he saw Omar approaching him with a sheet of paper. "Mr. Mayor here is the data you've requested. Sorry for the delay but we've just received it ourselves" Omar whispered and then turned to his seat.

Looking down at his cheat sheet, he began to read slowly. "We seized 96 guns, many fixed to fire automatically, and over 500 pounds of various drugs and narcotics, including cocaine, ecstasy, opiates, Fentanyl, and marijuana" he declared. "We now know that your team disrupted a major operation. The warehouse was going to be used to distribute all around the city by drones and ship by truck to neighboring cities and towns. Drones of all things. What the hell is the world coming to?" he asked, shaking his head.

"But all that went up in smoke, I'm happy to say. We arrested some 57 gang members or more and turned them over to the district attorney. They're all being held on various charges, and with luck they'll be off the streets for quite some time. Anything you'd like to add, Omar?"

"Yes, sir, and thank you. In addition, the ring leader, AJ's cell phone had loads of incriminating evidence and the FBI is going over it now with Homeland Security. They have a line on AJ's contacts and I can't get into any more than that. I probably shouldn't even be telling you this much, but you deserve to know. This operation was a success because of the cooperation between us, the FBI, fire and rescue, and SWAT. I thank each and every one of you, so please stay awhile and enjoy," he said, while motioning the mayor to follow him to the back of the room.

"Mr. Mayor, here are the three kids I was telling you about. Miles, Katie and Ralph, and these are their parents."

The Mayor looked like he was hoping to pick up some votes in the next election. "This city owes the three of you a great debt of gratitude for your community service," he bellowed. "As a small token, we would like to give you these three brand new drones that were never unwrapped in yesterday's war," he smiled, pointing to three packages on the table.

The trio dove eagerly into the boxes and began putting the devices together eagerly. The Mayor simply smiled and continued his speech. "Now, unfortunately, it all must be kept within these confines. For your own safety, nobody else can know about your work for us. But rest assured, we all know that we could not have gotten through without your uh, kick-ass flying," he declared. The room erupted in laughter; Liz blushed deeply.

The Mayor reached into his coat pocket. "If I may, Miles I have a letter to present to you."

Miles just stood there looking at Ralph and Katie, who also stopped fiddling with their new drones. "Open it up," Katie insisted, while she leaned closer. "Read what it says."

Miles looked at his dad, who was smiling, so he knew it had to be something good. Turning the envelope over and looking at the return address, it read Department of Defense US Air Force. While grasping one corner, he quickly tore open one end of the envelope. As he reached inside for the contents, everyone held their breath with anticipation.

Slowly Miles pulled the letter out, staring at the words, but they seemed to be out of focus. Taking a deep breath, he began. "To Mr. Miles Watson, your initial query about professional positions within the Air Force was brought to our attention with follow-up from Mr. Omar Johnson and your city's Mayor, the Honorable Charles Hansen. With approval from both U.S. Senators representing your great state, it is my pleasure to inform you that you have been accepted for initial Flight Training School, Pueblo, Colorado, starting this October."

Miles just stood there speechless, while Katie reached over awkwardly and gave him a hug. Ralph spun his wheel chair around a couple of times. Miles just stared at his dad, the Mayor, Katie, and Ralph.

Miles pictured himself flying a Stealth fighter, or a screaming X-wing fighter from his favorite movie. Finally, he realized his manners. "Thank-you very much Mr. Mayor," he said, still a little lost.

"You're very welcome, Miles," Mayor Hansen said, shaking his hand.

"Guess you'll really be flying something bigger than drones huh, son?" Omar offered with a big wide smile as Katie and Ralph gave each other high fives.

"Or maybe not?" Omar reached into his pocket and produced another letter addressed to Miles. This one was from Terrestrial Systems. "I was holding for you, but forgot to give it to you with all the recent excitement," he announced, while extending his arm.

Miles was about to put the envelope into his pocket when Ralph rolled closer. "Go ahead, open it. It's probably just a bill."

Omar just glared at Ralph but held his remarks to himself, as he nodded to Miles to open the contents.

With a deep breath, Miles fished out the letter from the envelope and read a few sentences in silence, then looked at everyone puzzled. With the urging of Katie, Miles began to read aloud. "To Miles Watson, We at Terrestrial Systems would like to offer you a position in our advanced technology division as a paid intern. As you may already know, Terrestrial Systems has developed and continues to develop aerial drone delivery systems for global customers. This exciting enterprise is leading tomorrow's technology today, and we'd like to have you on our team. This position carries with it the ability to attend engineering college, fully paid."

Miles just looked at Katie, Ralph, his dad and the Mayor, then smiled at his mother and even his little brother.

"How did Terrestrial Systems know about you, Miles?" Ralph asked.

"I don't know. Maybe they've been following me at the races."

"Or maybe at the High School job fair we all had to attend," Ralph continued. "So, now what you gonna do?" Ralph inquired.

"I know what I'd do," Katie joined in. "After what we just went through, there's no way I'd go into the military to fly anything. No more drone deaths for me," she said with authority.

Then there was silence as everyone awaited Miles' decision, but all he did was shake his head in confusion.

Breaking the awkwardness, the Mayor turned from Miles and looked at Ralph with a with a wide grin. "Here is an envelope for you, too," he said. Ralph began to open the envelope slowly and in anticipation began to hum *Pushing Mach 5.* Slowly he slid the letter from its envelope and broke out with a wide grin.

"What does it say?" Katie inquired.

"It says I've been hired as an instructor by the police department, rather the academy. Going to teach new recruits to fly drones!" With that, he thanked the Mayor and spun his wheel chair around a couple of times, giving his dad a high-five and enduring a hug from his mom. Everyone then looked at Katie, feeling somewhat guilty and embarrassed that she hadn't received anything yet.

As if on cue, she looked back at everyone, then smiled at her parents. With both thumbs pointed to her T-shirt, she smiled. "Like it says, MY SEX CAN BEAT YOUR SEX --DRONE JUNKY." This caused both her mother and father to blush openly at her boldness. "But I'm done racing drones. I was going to tell you guys, but we got caught up in the war. Anyway, first I have a little something for the both of you," she said while reaching down into her back pack. She pulled out two T-shirts, one for Miles and the other for Ralph. Each had their names on it and underneath it read, "FRIEND OF KATIE".

Katie looked at Miles, then at her mom. "So here's my announcement. I've been accepted into medical school. I'm going be a surgeon!" she said proudly. "Maybe I can invent a way to steer little tiny drones into someone's heart and fix it," she said with a laugh.

Ralph snickered. "Oh, going for the big bucks in the private sector!" he teased. She just rubbed her right thumb and forefinger together with a haughty grin.

As the laughter died down, Katie looked at the new drones and smiled. "Well, better keep in practice," she laughed. "Anyone up for a little flying lesson?" she challenged, while picking up a drone.

"I'm in," Ralph replied, turning on his transmitter while smiling at Katie.

"I'm in, too," Miles laughed enthusiastically. Then he looked at Omar. "No, I mean I'm in the private sector, too. I'm not going into the military. Kendra said she'll never forget what she saw overseas, during her tour of duty. I thought that being a military pilot was what I wanted to do, but now I don't think that's for me."

Looking at the Mayor, he fought for the appropriate words. "I'm sorry Mr. Mayor but I can't go into go to Colorado. My skills will be better used at Terrestrial Systems," he declared, while staring at Omar. "Besides, my Dad did tell me to get a damned job!" he added with a smile.

Omar and Bernestine proudly smiled back. "Son, I'd say you've more than earned the right to make your own decisions about your future. We're with you, whatever you decide."

The team finished assembling their drones and placed them on a makeshift starting line. Miles motioned to Kenny to slide open a large a window and turned to the mayor. "Mr. Mayor, one last request. Would you please do the honors of our final count down, from five?" he asked politely while sliding the window open.

The mayor nodded, and with a booming voice, he called out the sequence. "Five, four, three, two, one, GO!"

The three drones rose simultaneously and darted through the window, with Kenny leading the entire room in humming the *Pushing Mach 5* theme.

CPSIA information can be obtained
at www.ICGtesting.com
Printed in the USA
FFHW020806110819
54165659-59908FF